I Dream Of Mirrors

Chris Kelso

'Kelso is a fearless and accomplished prose stylist.'
– Ray Nessly, Literary Orphans

'Chris Kelso writes in a style of broken glass and razor blades, barbed wire and gasoline. Stitching together prose, poetry, drama, and graphic novel in a Frankenstein aesthetic...'
– John Langan, author of The Wide, Carnivorous Sky and Other Monstrous Geographies

'I think Kelso is a major talent and you'll hear more about him as time goes by. However, his work is not for the squeamish. His work is transgressive, erudite, shocking.'
– Mary Turzillo, NEBULA winner

'Chris Kelso is a writer of almost intimidating intelligence, wit, and imagination. On every page there is evidence of a great mind at work. Just when you're wondering if there are actually still writers out there who still feel and live their ideas out on the page, I come across a writer like Kelso, and suddenly the future feels a lot more optimistic. One calls to mind Burroughs, and Trocchi's more verbose offerings - whilst remaining uniquely himself, in a writer as young as he is, is a very encouraging sign: one of maturity that belies his youth. I look forward to reading more from him in the near future.'
— Andrew Raymond Drennan, author of the Immaculate Heart

'Chris Kelso is an important satirist, I think it's safe to say.'

— Anna Tambour, author of Crandolin

'Someday soon people will be naming him as one of their own influences.'

— INTERZONE magazine

'Come into the dusty deserted publishing house where mummified editors sit over moth-eaten manuscripts of books that were never written...anyone who enjoys the work of my late friend William Burroughs will feel welcome here with Chris Kelso.'

— Graham Masterton

'Chris Kelso's prose swaggers like blues and jitters like bebop. Dig.'

— Nate Southard, author of Down and Just Like Hell.

'Kelso steams with talent and dark wit and his blend of anarchy with precision is refreshing, inspiring and utterly entertaining . . .'

— Rhys Hughes, author of Mister Gum

'Choke down a handful of magic mushrooms and hop inside a rocket ship trip to futuristic settings filled with pop culture, strange creatures and all manner of sexual deviance.'

— Richard Thomas, author of Transubstantiate

Further reading by the Sinister Horror Company:

THE CHOCOLATEMAN – *Jonathan Butcher*
WHAT GOOD GIRLS DO – *Jonathan Butcher*

MARKED – *Stuart Park*

HELL SHIP – *Benedict J. Jones*

MR. ROBESPIERRE – *Daniel Marc Chant*
INTO FEAR – *Daniel Marc Chant*
DEVIL KICKERS – *Daniel Marc Chant & Vincent Hunt*

CORPSING – *Kayleigh Marie Edwards*

FOREST UNDERGROUND – *Lydian Faust*

THE UNHEIMLICH MANOEUVRE – *Tracy Fahey*

KING CARRION – *Rich Hawkins*
MANIAC GODS – *Rich Hawkins*

DEATH – *Paul Kane*

THE BAD GAME – *Adam Millard*

TERROR BYTE – *J. R. Park*
PUNCH – *J.R Park*
UPON WAKING – *J. R. Park*
THE EXCHANGE – *J. R. Park*
POSTAL – *J. R. Park & Matt Shaw*
DEATH DREAMS IN A WHOREHOUSE – *J. R. Park*
MAD DOG – *J. R. Park*

GODBOMB! – *Kit Power*
BREAKING POINT – *Kit Power*

Visit SinisterHorrorCompany.com for further information on these and other titles.

SINISTER
HORROR
COMPANY

PRESENTS

CHRIS   KELSO

I   DREAM

OF

MIRRORS

I Dream Of Mirrors

Edited by J. R. Park
Interior design by Daniel Marc Chant & J. R. Park
Cover design by Michael Bray

Published by The Sinister Horror Company

I Dream Of Mirrors -- 1st ed.
ISBN 978-1-912578-07-8

Art / photography by Shane Swank.

For Denise.

Chris Kelso

RULES OF THE PEOPLE

ONE

The People, as a group led by Miles Dunwoody, prohibit the making of any law respecting an establishment of religion, impeding the freedom of speech, infringing on the freedom of the press, interfering with the right to peaceably assemble or prohibiting the petitioning for a governmental redress of grievances – unless it is deemed exception by Miles Dunwoody.

'It is not down on any map; true places never are.'
— **Herman Melville, Moby-Dick**

My bones feel new, brittle. You won't have heard any apocryphal stories about me because no one seems to know anything about me. My body is a sheet of paper from a worn manuscript, folded into the origami shape of a man. My life has been stuffed into a satchel. Carried to publishers and rejected by the majority. Its words are my words.

This begs the question – *who is the author?*

3

I look down to the shuffling horde. I see the sun catch the corner of a skyscraper, whip it into a golden prism before sending it straight into the watery eye of the street-bound beholder. I watch them staring, transfixed by the light, a Clockwork Orange amid forced aversion therapy. Always searching for something. I look at my own hands, dry as rough-cast.

I suppose I've been searching for something too. I hope my story is kind of like Ahab's.

One –

'I began with the Imaginary, I then had to chew on the story of the Symbolic ... and I finished by putting out for you this famous Real.'
- Jacques Lacan

I've concluded that happiness lives in the ephemera. You cannot see it, nor can it be considered tangible. It's not quite an optical illusion – no, not quite – but if you *try* to catch it, with the ultimate intention of somehow sustaining it for a prolonged period, then happiness will quickly dissolve to grief and disappointment – *inevitably, fatally.*

This may seem like a redundant observation, but you'll forgive me for being a little behind. Re-learning how to survive, how to kill and love is one thing, but remembering all the old cynicisms that really make you human, well, that's a completely different process altogether.

Kad and I stand on the roof of the old convenience store, loading up a spear gun - really, she does all the work since I lost four of my fingers when a shotgun exploded in my hands because of an obstructed barrel. That's a story for another time.

Daytime has left us. Even at night, the uniform newness of the city sparkles, surreal and blue, against midnight's cape. For us dwellers of the dark, bathed in the cities lustre, it makes fighting back a little easier when the light goes. Kad grips the handle of the weapon with her left hand, wedges the butt against her chest, reaches over with her right hand and yanks the elastic towards the notch of the spear. She grunts under the forced exertion.

'They're coming!' – I warn her, clutching the bag of supplies we just looted.

I hear the cable click into the spear notch. She takes aim, pointing downwards into the oncoming horde. I can hear Kad's breath escape in heavy gasps. I know she is nervous because the bracelets on her left hand are clanking against the speargun barrel with barely-contained energy. Fuck, my heart is going like a bursting bug in my throat. I don't think it's ever pumped this hard before.

Keep it together, *come on*.

In the distance I see shadows crawling like starving insects over the solar panel-clad co-operative buildings and the bird-nest villas that come to a cluster on the mountainside. I used to live there, but that seems like the longest fuckin' time ago.

'Fire!' – I yell, clutching the grocery bag into my chest as two of the motherfuckers climb up onto the burnt-out skeleton of a Ford Escort to get a better pedestal to the convenience store roof. Kad still hasn't fired. I turn to her. The breathing has slowed down now, her hand seems steadier around the barrel. Good.

'Fire!' – My voice cracks with anxiety, I see the extra octave shudder along her vertebrae.

- I'm breaking her concentration.

Yet I can't help myself. I'm practically hysterical. Kad remains hesitant, still aiming. Smoke works up from the vent pipe in a churning vortex, blending the midnight blue with its grey tincture. Eventually, Fear eats up my patience.

'Fucking fire!' – And, finally, the rubber snaps and a harpoon spear arrows straight into a stack of gas canisters which explode on impact, popping one after the other like Chinese firecrackers would. It's like something out of a movie. The exploded barrels send a spray of flames and debris into the crowd. Their bodies disperse throughout the forecourt.

'Fuck, good shot…'

'Maybe next time you'll get off my case when it comes to pulling the trigger.' – Kad grins as she seizes another spear and starts loading. The People who haven't been sautéed are drawn towards the jagged teeth of fire, away from our vantage point.

'I think we can go now. They're pulling back. Let's go!'

'Wait'

- Fucking wait?

Kad locks the cable into the spear notch. She retakes her aim and, this time, spares no hesitation before despatching a harpoon straight into the back of a flaming figure in a seersucker suit. She tears off an amber pendant from around her neck and throws it into the crowd.

'My ex…I *think*'

***

The abandoned Aerial Hotel is one of the highest buildings in the city, higher even than the skyscrapers and co-operatives. Its stilts are made from reinforced concrete pilings and project the building 295 stories high above the Schism. Ours is a city with buildings so tall and resplendent that they almost defy human ingenuity. 'The giant's playground' - I mean, how insignificant are we *meant* to feel when the shortest office building is 1,722 feet from street-level? It doesn't seem to matter to anyone. No one gives a shit. Apathy rules. Now there's just a copper pang of blood in the air, a vague almondy aroma of bone and primal rot…

- *anyway. I digress.*

Unlike the other structures here, the Aerial Hotel isn't comprised of steel or mirror-glass - it's made from sun-baked brick and is shaped like a terraced step pyramid of successively receding levels. Kad and I have sought refuge here. It appears to be the most isolated building available. Believe me, we've been looking for a long time. It certainly feels like a long time.

Kad is determined to tear down every poster of Miles Dunwoody she sees, no small task given the aggressive marketing campaign conducted by his followers. She's almost completely rid the Aerial Hotel of his effigy – until, we arrive in the lobby, and Kad suddenly veers off to the reception desk where she hurdles the counter and rips away a poster of the saviour's sinister sneer from the back wall.

'I *hate* that cunt's face!' – She spits and wipes the excess drool from the corner of her mouth with one swipe of her wrist.

- *You do not hate his face.*

'I know you do.' – I say.

Kad goes prowling for more portraits to deface. My beleaguered eyes narrow at the silverbright. Head towards the light.

I watch her tassel of dark hair disappear into the half-light like a mirage.

The People aren't undead you understand, no, they are merely the devoted followers of a wealthy psychopath called Miles Dunwoody – a 39 year old real estate heir who pumped all his grandfather's hard-earned cash into forming *The Schism*. The modern zombie is kind of like your classic fundamentalist; always searching, evermore consumed, and driven even, by primal instincts of self-preservation and a *need* to belong. *Aah*, what it is to belong, eh? There must be a destination (*must* be). Collectively, they call themselves *The People*. They are complete morons.

They do possess some outline of self, can rationalise within the limitations they have provided themselves, but, ultimately, they are misguided in their pursuit. Ready martyrs, blind disciples. Or they might just be complete morons.

As if it's ever that simple.

Now, The Schism is what we call the naked streets of our fair city, the streets transformed by a religious cult that places Dunwoody at the centre as its messiah. It's ironic, his relatives virtually built this city, designed it, so his empire has deep foundations.

Like all cult religions though, the specifics are a little sketchy. I'll try and break it down for you as best I can. Here's the gist of their philosophy, so do pay attention: Like many a supervillain, Dunwoody plays on our fetish for freedom; he claims that *he* is the chosen vessel, that we are *all* children of Light at perpetual war with the powers of darkness and the city should be divided up into seekers of the light (the morons) and dwellers of the dark (the damned).

So, yes, he's a fucking madman.

Kad and I are both dwellers of the dark, and proud of it - not proud of it exactly, but we've embraced it. It's the only facet of my identity that I can truly claim.

People like Kad and I were not susceptible to his transmission.

Our army marches on its stomach.

'Look at this cunt. How can people be so fucking stupid?' – Kad comes back through the half-light holding up a shredded poster of Dunwoody in the air.

'Ahh, the power of coercive persuasion! I think it involves the systematic breakdown of a person's sense of self.' – What the fuck do I know? I don't even have any memories.

'Come on. There must be more going on here. Call me an optimist, but I refuse to believe that the residents of this city would be collectively so dumb. The transmission was so lame. So phony.'

'He's charming and…I don't know, I suppose Dunwoody *is* an attractive man. He was considered the silver fox of the property market.'

Kad kinks her face up in disgust.

'No way, he looks like a creepy bastard.'

'Come on. You're saying that, if you didn't know him, you wouldn't let him spend a night at Casa De Kad?'

She gawks her eyes at me, strained in active loathing.

'Not even if he paid me in advance for the pleasure.'

- *Yeah right.*

Kad is stubborn but I know that there *must* be a lingering attraction to Dunwoody. Call me suspicious but…

On many occasions, in our drunken weekends cooped up in the Aerial Hotel, Kad has confessed her love for high-profile men; for yuppies, economists and chartered management accountants with mistresses and villas in the Balearics. Her last two boyfriends since the Schism were a Civil Service fast streamer and a financial risk analyst, both with cotton white hair and wideflung shoulders compressed into expensive suits. Mirror images of Dunwoody.

So, okay, yes, Dunwoody *is* a beautiful man by most people's standards, with oodles of charm and charisma to boot. I think this is what annoys Kad the most - she hates these men with all the sincere fiery passion of her womanhood but is uncontrollably drawn to them. I won't push her on this though, comparisons are odious, and I've seen Kad with a speargun!

We sit in the lounge and empty the contents of the grocery bag onto a glass table - a dozen cans of non-perishable food, bandages, a bow-saw with an extra blade, 4-mil polyethylene film, a homemade shelter-ventilating pump, 1kg of Formula B rat poison, large containers for water and a dozen bottles of sodium hypochlorite bleach.

'Fucker.' – Kad curses the air, punches the table with a closed fist. The items rattle on the glass surface.

'What's wrong?' – I ask.

'We forgot the energy drinks…' – her head collapses into her hands.

'Shit. We forgot the rope too.' - I adjoin unhelpfully.

'I bought us some rat-poison. We won't need a rope.'

Then, there is a clattering coming from the little coffee shop beside the front-desk. I suddenly become aware of how breakable my bones feel. How stressed out my heart must be. My gut swirls like a waterspout.

Squelch *Squelch*

'Wait…do you hear that?'

A noise…wet shoes squishing on a flat-weave carpet. Kad and I lay in wait for the source to present itself, paralysed by fear and anticipation. The sound gets closer, louder, and other noises are distinguished in its proximity – the sound of groaning, desperate and hungry, freezes a block of ice in my chest. The Aerial Hotel has never been infiltrated before.

Squelch *Squelch*

They must've found our hatchway.

What am *I* supposed to do in this situation? With four fingers on my good hand I couldn't even jack my own dick to a satisfying conclusion. I look at Kad who is starting to slowly inch towards the bone-saw resting on the glass table.

Squelch *Squelch!* *Squelch!!* *SQUELCH!*

The noise is almost in the same room as us. I can hear it all now. Rotten teeth grinding to dust, a remote-controlled mind living out its own delusion.

The ugly motherfucker shuffles into view, a man wearing a red t-shirt with Miles Dunwoody's universally merchandized and objectified image on it. The zombie has these big, pleading eyes that are in stark contrast to what you'd expect from the intellectually, emotionally castrated.

'You…both of you…' – it mutters and points reprovingly. Kad rises to her feet, bone-saw clutched in her hand like a lumberjack ready to tackle a king Beech. She takes one look at Dunwoody's face on the t-shirt and charges at the shambling sleepwalker. Her shock of black hair trails in her wake like a superhero's cape.

'Kad, wait!' – But it's too late, she's on top of the poor moron.

SCHUNK!

A spray of red pollen fills the air, moans become shrieks of tortured agony. I hear bone branches break, a tearing of the sinew as Kad yanks a limb from its owner and tosses it aside.

'Wait! I just wanted to…' – the zombie tries to talk but it'll do no good. Hell hath no scorn like a dark dweller's instinct for survival.

Kad goes back for more, hacking and tearing at the hard bark, a foaming geyser of arterial fluid sprouts from the delicate stem of a ruptured neck vein.

'No, please! *No------*' – the voice trails off. I can virtually smell the adrenaline spiking in Kad's bloodstream. The king Beech has been conquered. When the squirming ceases, Kad stands up covered in sap. She looks at me.

'How *the fuck* did it get in here?'

'I don't know. The hatchway?' - I walk over to the corpse. He's wearing espadrilles, a trench coat and has no shirt on underneath. His trousers are torn at the knees and he looks like he may have once been an out of work actor. I lean forward and take in his stink, breathe it deeply into my lungs. Even in death, he reeks of happiness.

'Didn't you close it behind you?' – Kad accuses.

'I…' – suddenly it hits me. I *didn't* close the fucking hatch behind me. Guilt swells up in my throat, my remaining fingers are puffy with inflated blood.

'I…don't think I closed the hatchway…'

Kad looks upon my confession like a catholic mother who just caught her only son reading some forbidden heretical literature. Light gilds her cheekbones and brow in an ominous fashion. Fuck, here it comes. I'm about to be summarily dismissed.

'Didn't we set up rules? Were you unclear about your role?'

'No…I just forgot.'

Kad makes an exasperated sound.

'You know you have to…'

'I know…'

- I know.

I can already feel my memory try to eternalise her, grasp at the fading splendour of her face. I hear the metal drawer she keeps her pistol in slide open. A round is chambered, hammer cocked. Kad thumbs the safety and lets me know…not that I don't *already* know.

I pack up my stuff and prepare to leave the Aerial Hotel. My desertion of duty is the worst kind of betrayal. I feel the depth of her pain in the rests of my soul. How could I be so fucking stupid? *Devil take the hindmost*, as Kad always says.

'I'm sorry. Sincerely, please don't…that is…*fuck*…'

She nods, accepting the apology but damning me with an expression of military coldness.

'You keep the stuff Kad, the poison and the other provisions. I can always loot more.'

'Thank you.'

'Single finger discount.' - I hoist my deformed claw, hoping to provide some levity to proceedings, but she's having none of it.

- Good one, asshole.

I depart shamed and I can hardly blame the girl for exiling me to the Schism. I could've gotten us both killed. In a world like this, survival *always* takes precedence. There is no room for sympathy or second chances. Death is also a pointless option. What lies beyond this place could be ten times worse. Better the devil you know and all that…

We are the dwellers in the dark. I must outrun the light on my own now. Like in those Russian novels I never read…

Chris Kelso

Two -

'The face is the mirror of the mind, and eyes without speaking confess the secrets of the heart.'

- St. Jerome

I am always giving permanent thumbs up.

A linocut poster of Miles Dunwoody imposes the cityscape. I look back at the tripod of the gravity defying Aerial Hotel and think of Kad one final time. Of my latest in a long line of fuck ups. Now I've been banished, the hotel looks even more romantic – it's pale blue glow, serene and hypnotic. Such awesome symmetry.

It was only a matter of time I guess.

I stick to the shadows cast in the wake of the giant cylindrical towers illuminated by LED lights. Various odours drift in and out of reception – blood, sweat, petrol and axel grease. The night is filled with moaning and indistinct chanting.

I think it's a good thing I found Kad, or I wouldn't be alive today. Not just because she's handy with a speargun, but she doesn't think twice about killing another human-being if her life is in danger. I on the other hand, well, I struggle. I haven't notched up a single fatality since the transmission. It's the eyes, they seem so full of hope and life, narrowing off in an epicanthic fold. I wonder how long I'll last. How long can a man with empathy for his hunters last? I imagine not that long.

A spume of blood lines the streets beneath my feet.

The People roam the spiral, glass-covered skywalk above, searching for detractors of Miles Dunwoody.

- *That fucker.*

I worry about being sucked into this shared fantasy. It was easy when I had someone else around to give me perspective, someone strong-minded and resilient – but I'm alone now and, I gotta admit, I'm not all that strong-minded. By my own admission I'm naïve and gullible. What if Dunwoody manages to convince me with another transmission? It stands to reason that if people are intrinsically irrational and stubborn, tired and afraid of living in a hopeless world, then they will follow any old harbinger of hope.

What if he comes after his cynics personally? After all, if the mountain will not come to Mohammed, then Mohammed must go to the mountain, right?

You know, the city was once known for its eco-consciousness and ingenious planning. It's true. In fact, the Dunwoody family pioneered various initiatives to *help* our environment. They increased vehicle prices and introduced a computer system that carefully analysed cab usage so that emissions could be kept low.

I think Miles Dunwoody senior would be appalled by his son's actions if he were alive today.

Escaping the city is something of a challenging, if not *completely* unachievable, task. There seems to be no other place in the world. It's like nowhere else exists. We can see beyond the city limits – just about - but it seems to fade into darkness, even during the daytime. As if the light from Dunwoody's architecture is the only light in the world somehow. I never wanted to leave though, never even thought about it.

What did I do before the fall of our great city?

I think I worked with my hands, maybe an artist. Maybe a mechanic. I manipulated things with my hands, back when I had two of them. It's almost like…I just can't really remember….

Then - I hear people. Mutterings of a conversation. I slide through the shadows and into an alleyway. I see three silhouettes crouching beside a dumpster. They turn to me and there is a pregnant pause, like when feral animals cross paths in the wild.

'Who's there?' – One of them asks in a thick street-accent.

'Please, I'm human, a dark dweller, don't panic.' – The three silhouettes stand up at the same time and motion towards me like synchronised dancers, swimming through the void. The palms of my feet start sweating.

'Come into the half-light.' – The same voice instructs. I obey and move deeper into the alleyway. A drowning man will clutch at a fucking straw.

'I've been cast out. Cast out of my hiding place. I have no friends, no allies. Please, can I maybe tag along with you guys? I don't know how long I'll last out here on my own.'

- I do. Not long.

In the gathered half-light of the backstreet I see the illumined faces of two men and a young woman.

The men are both African-American, panther-esque, too alike not to be brothers. Both are big, burly with equally massive shoulders and matching facial tattoos on their brows – an ancient hieroglyph that I can't quite place despite the cloud of information at my disposal.

19

The woman has the same tattoo on her neck and is small, skinny, seems barely a teenager. She reminds me of a puppy or a kitten. Her black hair flows and disappears into the glooms around her. She glances at the misshapen flesh-hook resting by my right side. It's okay, I'm not self-conscious.

'We're conducting a spell.' – the girl reveals, placing herself in front of the two men, as if protecting them from any potential threat I might pose. I see that the three of them are wearing brass gloves with jagged teeth protruding from the knuckles that extend as far as the cuticle – an ingenious ad hoc weapon to assist individual human survival during these wayward times.

'What kind of spell?' – I ask.

'It's too soon to tell you. Do you believe in the Key?' – She squints at me, trying to figure me out at face value.

'What's that?'

'The Key of the Nile' – she points to her neck tattoo and the two men point to theirs.

- *Christ...*

'If you're not part of Dunwoody's cult then you're friends of mine.' – I say this hoping I haven't just stumbled across *another* batshit cult. They seem like a shifty bunch, hanging out in the dusks and chanting stupid curses - but then I'm reminded that most people wander this city like famished ghosts these days. It's hard to tell friend from enemy.

'This is Rat, this is Velm. My name is Ursula. We are healers.'

'Healers of what?'

'Of the plague that befell this city. We are masters of psychic surgery, it's our mission to alleviate the Dunwoody hex.'

'Future life, life after death! Verse 295.' – Velm adds somewhat redundantly.

'And it works?'

Ursula looks at Rat and Velm.

- Didn't think so.

'We *have* to believe it works. Otherwise, there is no hope. If there is no hope, then what's the point? We might as well join the brainwashed.'

So, it's faith they're after too. What is it with this city? Why does everyone have to get so crazy for divine intervention? And what's with those brass claws? Surely if they're so powerful they don't need weapons? Maybe I'm being too harsh on them, everyone has the right to protect themselves. I think I'm just green-eyed cos I don't have a pair of those gloves to hide my hook.

'But, can't we just form a resistance and assassinate the fucker?'

Ursula snorts.

'No one has seen Dunwoody in person in years. He's an apparition. The only way to get to him is through ancient spells.'

'I see.' – She seems to have disavowed the obvious fact that Dunwoody is ominously present even in his absence.

- These guys are just full of excuses.

The girl, Ursula, is clearly a runaway caught up in the wrong crowd. The other two? Ex-gangbangers I imagine.

She reaches through the darkness, I feel her hand on mine. Her flesh is soft and warm in the frozen night and her eyes are rich with desire. She could make a believer of most men. The tenderness of Ursula's touch tricks me into following her through the shades.

The hulking presence of Velm and Rat narrow the parameters of the alleyway to a crushed rectangle. They survey me with an innate hostility.

We crouch to the same spot on the concrete where I first found them. There's an eye drawn on the ground in blue talc. Ursula traces the eye, drags her brass talon through the powder and makes it weep.

'Imhotep, god of medicine and healing. He is our only figure of worship, and we worship his mind, not his holy powers.'

'Seems fair. So, is there an incantation or something we need to recite?'

- I can't believe I just said that…

'*We?*'

'Yes, I'd like to help if I can.'

Velm appears before me, kneeling, with an intense stare that seems capable of penetrating the shrines of my most private thoughts. I can't stop looking at his tattoo, at the rusted spikes of his gloves, the gloves that make all three of these kids seem like rabid, unchained animals.

I *need* a pair of those damn gloves. This is about survival. I learned that from Kad.

Velm speaks.

'You can't help man, ain't nobody can do this who ain't been branded, ya see?'

'So, what? You need to prove yourself to get branded?'

He nods.

- Fuck off.

'Prove myself? I mean, I thought we were all on the same team here?'

- Evidently not.

'Nah man, there are a lot of factions in this city, a lot of

People sympathisers, a lot of crazy motherfuckers who can't deal with the end of civilised society.'

'I'm not a fuckin' sympathiser, I hate Dunwoody and what he's done. I don't think I'm crazy either…*yet* anyway.'

Velm stands up, looms over me, and arches his spine with both sets of talons spread out by his side as if ready to lunge-attack. He snarls and shows his gums and golden crown caps.

'I don't like this guy, Ursula…he reeks of The People and the beast.'- He condemns with mulish scorn.

Ursula stands up, places a delicate palm on his hulking chest.

'Velm, we have to give him the chance to prove himself. People can change. We can't just toss him aside like you did with Fiona, with Ailsa. We're not about senseless brutality. We're witches. That's not how we do business.'

Rat huffs from somewhere in the dark alleyway, out of view.

- Jesus…

'I'm with Velm man, I say we ditch the invalid. All we got is each other. We ain't a coven yet…'

- Fuckin…

'And the reason we ain't a coven is because we never give anyone else a chance to join! You think I saw you both and didn't think twice about…you guys were nothing before I taught you about…' – Ursula doesn't finish her sentence. Rat responds from the darkness.

'Hey, you don't know *who* we were before this. You don't know who *you* were before it either. You coulda been a goddamned…'

- Christ…

I interrupt with a hand gesture. I don't have time for silly kids' games or their bickering.

'Listen guys, don't fight, please. I don't much fancy being branded or having to prove myself anyway. I'll move along, okay, let you get on with your hocus pocus.'

I squeeze past Rat, back out into the bloody street carnival. I pick up the stink of epoxy resin from him.

'Wait…'

Ursula appears. I feel warm, delicate flesh overturn my right hand, facing the palm to the sky.

'If you're leaving, at least take this…' – Ursula slides off her right glove and shoves it into my hand. It weighs a ton.

'It'll give you protection. You'll need it. It might help you prove a point one day.'

'Thank you. I hope your spell works, really, I hope it works.'

The city is a cage bursting with roaring, tormented animals. The city is alive with purulent cries. She's out there somewhere, Kad, deep in that abyssal, serrated outline of the cityscape.

The man who stole my reflection – face solemn and drawn, eyes like swirling vortexes of misery. He's a burnt-out shadow of a man and it's impossible to conceal these facts given the extent of his physical squalor.

The transmission tower spears the sky. Bodies are flocking towards it and it's obvious Dunwoody is about to deliver his latest sermon…

Day - 3
Month - ?
Year - ?

*'One does not become enlightened by imagining figures of light,
but by making the darkness conscious. The latter procedure, however,
is disagreeable and therefore not popular.'*
— C.G. Jung

This is my first journal entry, my first contribution to the great airborne anthology of names and stories hovering over the city.

Being a shadow is a funny thing. You flit between the interstices of light all day long and try to project yourself as far as you can, like a shrill squillo over a loud orchestra. It's a lonely life - I don't think people appreciate that. I am merely a tracing on the wall, camera obscura.

Every day, for as long as I can remember, I have watched my light-brother, my sunny overhang, try his damndest to outrun me. Whenever I turn a corner, half expecting to come face to face with the man himself, he shifts into the nearest sunlit street. He does this because he knows I can't get him there. I'm like a time delay, always three seconds behind actual events. The lobotomised Kurt, who basks in the golden dawn, serene as an eagle, thinks me a coward. We can never be friends, he and I.

Now, his rejection hurts a lot, it does, but I think I understand it. He sees me and thinks *'Christ, that's a lonely, pathetic existence, eh? Loitering in alleyways, running scared all the time…lonely, unloved…no identity to speak of'* and he'd be right. The bliss found in ignorance, in belonging, is so seductive a prospect that to continually deny it becomes a maddening form of torture. My architect made me this way, made me resolute, made misery a part of who I am.

My light-brother, who has a full set of fingers on each hand and a happier frame of mind than most, knows if I got half a chance I'd consume him, *assume* him. I'd fill his heart with darkness and doubt; I'd kill the glimmer in his eye once and for all. I'd do it proudly, efficiently and with a broad smile on my face because the truth is I'm stronger than he is, even though he treads on me daily, hourly. *He's* the one who is always running.

Dazzling flames throw intensely dark shadows.

I'd make my light-brother remember every shitty thing that's ever happened to him since we both came stumbling into existence. Tattoo it on his soul so every time he looked in the mirror he'd be reminded of our story. Because I think he forgets.

But I know that no matter how much he seems to fight my existence, deny it, he *knows* we are intimately linked by a shatterproof bond, because - wherever there is light, there is darkness. He lusts for the darkness as much as I covet his inner glow.

I'm not special, shadows never are. *Everything* casts a shadow. The presence of a shadow does not even indicate the echo of something that's alive. After all, a fucking toaster casts a shadow. A corpse casts a shadow.

I'll keep dwelling in night, when everyone else is asleep. I'll hang out in places most people are too terrified to venture. Kad and I can survive if we bring our darknesses together.

I see names drift by, buried deep in the filaments of the cloud – Rick Deckard, The Shrike, Offred, Hari Seldon -

all men who have seen their own gods and were able to live a real life because of it. They are fictional characters, shadows, but are as real as their creators.

The great science fiction artwork of David Meltzer and Hannes Bokay float by in composed ice crystals....

A sheet of cirrostratus covers the sky. The names disappear and my head empties of all its retained contents. I remember something of the old world, before the city.

FIST

Every breath sounds
like the crumbling
of dry leaves. Eyes
dried, hollow socket
filled with searing
sand. Time no longer
unfolds but instead
unravels. A thousan
threads slicing like
piano wire through
pale white skin.

RULES OF THE PEOPLE

TWO

The People protect the right to keep and bear arms – as long as they are never turned on or used against any of The People members themselves.

Chris Kelso

Three -

'Our lives are full of all the genres. Fear and hope and sadness.'
- Nicolas Roeg

I feel that, somehow, my life alludes to all these fairy tales that are embedded in the collective conscious; specifically deriving from a genre you'd call 'science fiction'. There are all these names of writers looming over me, Philip. K. Dick, Samuel Delaney, Isaac Asimov, and Octavia Butler…all recorded in the filing cabinets of memory storage. The agglomerations hover spectrally in the atmosphere, floating in a shared pool of configurable computing resources.

I was born with these stories already in my head. I remember more from them than I do events in my own life. I am a prisoner of fiction. I use it to shape me.

But these stories, they're significant somehow. As if these are the writers of *my* story, of every story ever told or worth telling. Christ, it seems as if my life has been steeped in falsehood, boiled down to a series of tropes and clichés that I've been inextricably bound to in the process. Every day I meet a Dick Turpin or a Dr Benway - whoever *those* people are!

Well, whoever they are, I feel like they are important to the canon of literature inscribed on my limbic system.

I need to get off the streets, these macho streets. The beast wants to rape me. The sun is pumpkin-orange. Mournful plains beckon me. There is only ever the awful, unknowable present.

There are people, dark dwellers, having an open garage sale – sexual paraphernalia, guns, chains, their souls stuffed into gherkin jars, those sorts of thing. I take in the pheromones of fear that hang thick in the air. People can change.

Although I am a shy, withdrawn, incompetent man, I fancy my chances going it alone out here, more than with the three teenage witches in the alleyway. Dunwoody's face appears suddenly on the side of a glass monolith. The giant billboard screen lights up the streets, an electro-kinetic sculpture of the surname 'DUNWOODY' appears in a complex pattern of stainless steel planes and exposed superstructure.

The smell of liquid lard and gelatine makes itself apparent. This city does what it wants, when it wants. Or maybe I've got it wrong. Maybe it's a slave too, a prisoner of its own creator?

I walk towards the assembling crowd and smell the buddleia that has overrun the old railway lines. Dunwoody is making a steeple with his fingertips and resting his lips on his knuckles. He looks deep in thought, reporting to his herd from ziggurat-shaped living quarters.

I *need* to get off the fucking streets before he starts the transmission. I don't trust myself. Jesus, if I can't trust myself, where does that leave me? All I know is that I can't afford to hear his lecture. It threatens everything I am, the reality I *think* I trust.

Grinding metal and burnt paint, damp cloth…

Dunwoody opens his mouth to address the crowd.

'This message is for my little firecrackers who shun the light.'

My ears fold back. He's talking directly to me. Can he see me? If rumour is to be believed, he can see everyone, all the time. Dunwoody is omnipresent in the very fabric of this city.

'There are still so many of you who enthusiastically dwell in the darkness, who *choose* to hide from the true reality of things. I need to tell you about the insects. They're coming. None of the objects around you are your own. Your own body is not your own, not really. I have seen the real world, you would hate it. The BrainGate is as close to hell as you will find.'

- Careful, he can overhear my thoughts.

I catch the soft computerized inflection of his voice bleed into the chambers of my mind. I need to resist this. Dunwoody stands up and the camera pans back.

'Ailsa Bloom, you are a disabled monkey in that place. Can you believe that? Here you are a beautiful and capable, if stubborn, young firecracker. Kad C, you are merely a severed cat head hooked up to a hypercomputer. But here…'

Kad is a decapitated cat head? What the fuck must *I* be? Dunwoody keeps talking. I keep listening. Getting sucked in.

'You see, in the outside world, the scientists use this technique called intracortical brain–computer interface. I don't expect you to understand what I'm talking about, how could you?-but just listen. I am the only one who can go between worlds. I too am a man-made abomination, but I have managed to surpass the humans. The scientists *want* you to suffer, they want *us* to suffer, but I do not.

33

By implanting neurotrophic-cone electrodes into the subjects' brain they can induce any kind of reality they please. It's me who created this beautiful city for you all. I am the architect. They *want* you to dwell in the dark. I say we should make the most of this life, I can offer you happiness. True happiness. I am the computer virus that wants to help the inner circuitry rather than fry it.'

- A computer virus?

Then I see people vomiting this black treacle over themselves, onto the tarmac. I need to get off the fucking streets.

I'll go back to the Aerial Hotel, beg Kad to take me back. All I want is to be in her company again while all around me people choke on their own effluence.

Gargled animal noises fill the air. Howls and barking resound in the night's echo. Dunwoody looks straight at me from behind the screen.

So, am I just a Down syndrome chimp, or am I a man? I'm someone else's dream made flesh in the mind of a diseased animal?

- Maybe it's turtles all the way down.

Dunwoody starts talking again.

'I am the only decent cosmological argument my little firecrackers. I am the unmoved mover. Even though, when you really sit down and think about it, I supersede a Christian God in every aspect. I am transparent, I show you everything there is to be seen. Even the buildings are see-through. I provide answers, unlike God. I provide solutions, unlike God. I care, unlike any religious deity you care to name. You should also bear in mind that I am not responsible for your situation. I would never make my disciples miserable. That god is weak, he is an old man. I want you to enjoy this city, enjoy its unique haute couture food and clean air…'

I can't help but admire his power. Dunwoody is a master scam artist who uses his vast fortune to host elaborate demonstrations and create new means of thought reform that have effectively brainwashed over half the city. That's not easy! The zombies are victims of an induced dependency.

The internet explorer sign pops up on all the street signs.

I see a child, a young boy separated from the crowd. He gestures for me to follow him and runs towards a coffee shop, away from the gang of vomiting Dunwoody partisans.

I sneak off during the retch-fest and Dunwoody's fifty foot talking head follows me all the way.

***

The coffee shop is called JAVVA LOTUS and is an exceptional example of biomimicry. It has fluid, curved vectors that seem to fold in on themselves. I don't recall ever coming here for coffee.

It's empty when I enter, except for the young boy who is helping himself to a blue nitrogen ice-cream – and of course there's the customary visage of Miles Dunwoody staring back at me from every available wall in the establishment. I sit on the chair opposite the kid.

I read somewhere, I can't remember which magazine, that the in-store chairs of JAVVA LOTUS omit an electromagnetic field, designed to make the person sitting in them feel calm and centered.

Fuck, maybe Dunwoody really is our savior after all? Everything his family built or had commissioned seems to've been designed with the express purpose of *helping* the citizens of the city. That said, I don't feel any better than I did out there on the streets. Not really. I'm far too unsettled.

A robotic barista asks me if I'd like a flash-frozen alcoholic beverage. I tell him no. The chairs are ribbons of white plastic weaving out in continuous bands, plastic capillaries connecting the savior to his own innovations. I feel him watching me even now.

The kid laps at his blue cone. The backlit translucent Plexiglas behind him makes his outline glow. He is pale though, like he's never seen a red blood cell in his life. And his eyes are all puffy. I can't tell if he's been crying or if he's had an allergic reaction to something.

Outside I can hear the booms and chirps and cahs and growls of the various zombified citizens, turning the city into a mirror-glass jungle. *Perhaps* you could compare their fanaticism to an infection, an epidemic of the mindbody. This doesn't make them any less dangerous. Their moans fill the electric spectra of night like hideous creatures who have somehow managed to survive the abortion process and I'm reminded that human indoctrination is as powerful a weapon as any.

'Who are you?' – I eventually get out. He stares at me, protracting the silence to suit his infantile sugar craving.

'Who do *you* think I am mister?'

- Here we go again…

'I honestly have no idea.' – The kid slurps away until there is only a flattened peak of blue ice-cream hemorrhaging over the rim of the cone. He looks at me and talks.

'People are strange. We're all so scared and confused.'

'I'm not scared.' – He says confidently. I believe him.

'No? Well you're a braver man than I am.'

'It's better than the other place.'

'What other place?'

'The labs. The men poking around me. Even when I ask them to stop. The men aren't here anymore. They can't get me in this place, they can't mister, I checked.'

'You mean…the scientists?'

The kid nods in confirmation. Steam from his ice-cream has pooled at the ceiling of the coffee shop like swarming ghosts.

'Hey, listen, what's your name?'

'I don't have one. I've only been me for a couple of days. You don't have a name either mister.'

- *Why the little…*

'Listen kid, which side are you on? Be straight with me, come on. Why did you pull me into this coffee shop? Do you know about the light and the dark?'

He nods again but doesn't answer any of my questions.

'Hey, what happened to your hand mister?' – He asks, motioning towards my claw with his diminished ice-cream cone.

'An accident. I was playing with a very dangerous weapon.'

'No, you weren't. That's not how it happened.'

'Excuse me?'

'*They* did this to you too.'

'Who did?'

'The people in the lab.'

'You mean the scientists?'

He nods again.

'Someone tall with blonde hair and a foreign accent. He took a finger for each of your sins, 1, 2, 3, 4. There's someone who wants to talk to you mister. Someone important. He knows your name.'

The kid blinks at me in slow-motion. Something's not right. The smell of death tickles the recesses of my nasal cavity.

'Okay. Who? Who wants to talk to me?'

- Answer me you little fucker!

He keeps blinking his heavy lids at me. Suddenly, black tar starts leaking from each cavity he has to offer. It runs down his cheeks from the eye slits in liquid veins, from his mouth and from his nose and ears.

- Tell me this is another optical illusion?

I stand up and take a backwards stride. He's having some kind of seizure…then *talks*…

'Relax mister. You have a right to the truth and a right to happiness as well. You can be one of my little firecrackers.' – The voice emerging no longer belongs to the pale kid. It's Dunwoody. The Absolute Benefactor. His tone is almost machinelike, there is no trace of an accent. It emerges brisk and impersonal with all the charm you can expect from an ancient city's stale bureaucracy.

'You think I'm the bad guy, but I decided to use my virtual role as a real estate billionaire to provide a better world for the prisoners of the BrainGate…'

I inch forward. The image of the oozing child-vessel is distracting and upsetting.

'By creating the Schism? The People?' – I ask. A melanoid bubble forms and pops as the tar pours from the kid's maw in a ceaseless gush. He continues to talk through the spew of afterbirth.

'Yes. It is human nature to accept what is in front of them. The people here think they have lived life outside this city, but they haven't. There was never a time before coming here, only a false memory of other places. Just because you aren't really a person doesn't mean you should be denied the illusion of contentment. Don't you see, they *want* you to mistrust me! The only way I can get through to a human being is by making myself god. It's easier if things are just simple, black and white, good and bad. All this ambiguity, it leads to a kind of soul sickness. I made things easier. There is light, which is good, and dark which is bad. Infinite regress, when you overthink you diminish.' - His speech is so difficult to love, it seems incapable of expressing rich emotions - but his face and his confidence are alluring.

'If this is true, you've still done more harm than good. By creating a divide, the city is in fucking ruins. Here, you're either a brainwashed idiot or a starving nomad. You're *just* like the Christian god, *Miles*. At least he had the brass neck to be honest about things. We all know that cunt hates us.' – I almost can't believe my own balls, talking to this powerful entity like he's a dumb teenager. My hand is quaking, I better just calm down.

I'm sure he could eviscerate me in a fucking heartbeat if he felt like it. I'm way out of my league here.

'You think this world is so bad? Let me tell you something about this place. Two days ago this world was encased in flames, sunken in shadow and crawling with all the repellent creatures your collective nightmares could conjure…until *I* resurrected it, raised these beautiful skyscrapers to cast light where there never was any before. You wouldn't have lasted five minutes in the old place. It was a hedonist's paradise, full of aberrant sexual practices. You would've had to walk through the working-class cannibals of an H.G. Wells novels. I am hope, the only hope left in your world.'

'Then who am I?'

'An avatar. I estimate that you've probably been online in the BrainGate for about three days.'

'That's it?'

- That's it, eh?

'Thereabouts. Ever wonder why you can't remember much of your life before? You've only been a man for about three days, you've never fucked, never truly exorcised your intellectual thinking. Let me tell you something about man, and I'll relate this to the divide you see in the city now - Plato and Aristotle characterize *man* as driven by conflicting forces, you have a dual nature. You are as much driven by reason as the 'appetitive' aspect of man, desire, emotion. You want to be a man, well here is the constant struggle. The constant battle of reason and desire. This is what it is to be a man.'

'Am I a man?'

- A three day old man?

'I can't tell you that right now. You need to join me first, let me trust you. Walk by my side and help convert the others. I only need one thing from you. I need you to relinquish control, just a little bit. Enough to let me in. In time I will tell you everything about the real you, should you still desire that information. Sometimes ignorance is bliss.'

'And sometimes it's a fucking cancer.'

The kid's mouth opens, and a shriek emerges that shatters all eight-hundred light-diffusing glass panels in the floor of the JAVVA LOTUS. Covering my ears, I run through the exploding shards beneath me until I'm back outside.

A mob of maybe fifty brainwashed men and women have formed into waves, glowering at me with hunched spines and bloodless faces. Eyes leering like great periscopes and imbued with their sense of civic duty, the swarm of fanatics take chase.

Up above, where the mirror sentinels climb into the billows, I hear a screech like an alien instrument being untuned. The beast.

- The People are gathering … Isn't this ironclad proof he's telling the truth?

I am now terrified and convinced that Dunwoody will find me. The nocturnal light strikes off the flanks of the giant rectangles that reach skyward. Even a man's reflection can change. I look down at my hand and the fingers are gone. All of a sudden, I hear a woman's voice.

A familiar one.

Kad…

- I want to tell her I love her…but I am only allowed to think it.

I am the dying dreamer
Stuck in a perpetual ring
My castle is ever out of reach
I bet my happiness lives there

Day - 5
Month - ?
Year -

I recall that there was so much information out there. In fact, I can still feel it consuming everything and everyone right now. The beast never stops.

In the censored-city, our only access to the outside is through the cloud. Sometimes I feel safer here, with all the screeds of data smog and oversaturated pop culture references condensed to their basic minimum. I mean, the sheer amount of input to our system has long since exceeded our processing capacity. We all felt the same way. Spam and social media had taken over everything. I remember it, clear as day. The journalism of assertion, I remember it well too. We had all the information in the world at our fingertips, yet nobody knew anything. About as much as we know today.

People were beginning to shut down, retreat into themselves. Blogs and writing, music and films were everywhere – *every-fuckin'-where*. There was too much of everything. It killed art in the end. We started sinking in the mire of a bloated inbox, choking on its relentless glut. Fuck, we did it to ourselves.

A pertinent quote from a French philosopher drifts by –

- Of course it does…

'As long as the centuries continue to unfold, the number of books will grow continually, and one can predict that a time will come when it will be almost as difficult to learn anything from books as from the direct study of the whole universe. It will be almost as convenient to search for some bit of truth concealed in nature as it will be to find it hidden away in an immense multitude of bound volumes.'

The beast, it's comprised from all this data, its DNA is drenched in it. If things went back to the way they were before, before the filters, we'd be overwhelmed by it, overloaded. The beast comes from the outside world. It ruled the old world. We let it rule. We fed it and encouraged it to take our souls. In truth, the infobesity of the old world terrifies me today. I don't ever want to go back. But Kad does…that's what matters.

Chris Kelso

Four -

'You can't be idealistic in this world and not be crazy.'

- John Zorn

Christ…

I stare at my claw in the beatific moonshadow. My 5 o'clock shadow has come in heavy, I look a little like Captain Nemo. I feel duty bound to protect Kad. To get her out of this cul-de-sac city.

It never ends. Bodies contour the streets, their faces twisted into a Halloween-mask imitation of the saviour. I take in the street and see Ursula the teenage witch in her frock, standing awkwardly with both feet crushed into tight stilettos. Her hair cascades in whorls, eyes gaping like looking fish, black blood smeared all over her crooked little mouth like treacle.

. . . She looks older now. As if I needed a reminder that people change.

Ursula is in the middle of a group of zombies. They're waiting outside a truck sat on its axles. Inside are several humanoid morsels crying and praying for mercy, dark dwellers. Ursula looks like she's relishing it all and there's a middle-aged man dumb with fright. I keep expecting to wake up . . .

. . . Slide out of bed on a trail of my own sweat . . .

. . . Grope around for a switch to beat away the hideous light that's been cast across the face of the world . . .

But I never do wake up. No one loves me. I didn't realise how tough it was to be unloved in the world until I tasted love for myself and wanted nothing more than to give it.

Sometimes, when I think of Kad's face, of her perfect oval with its keen features, I see the ubiquitous Miles Dunwoody staring back at me instead. I don't know *why*. I can't explain it. I'm so used to seeing his appearance, I see it in the mirrors of my dreams. All I know is that this paranoia is a ravening limpet.

I've got to hold onto what I know. I can't forget who I am, who Kad is. I can't forget what we've been through together. She saved my life so many times.

Dunwoody is a psychotic. He is sick and wants us all to touch his devouring madness. I just need to remember, I just need to keep it in my head that none of us have to accept the same virus which has distorted *his* reality into our own lives. That would be insanity. Plus, Kad is here. She can give me some much-needed perspective.

I look back, see Ursula and the others lunge at their human feast, knocking over garbage cans and making some of the obscenest chewing noises I think I've ever heard. I can only see a bare human leg sticking out, calf flexed, and ankle drawn tight. A teardrop of semen unexplainably bleeds from the eye of my penis.

We hear something trying to connect, radio static carrying god. Dunwoody's frequency travels along the crests of waves.

The corrosion-resistant skyscraper kills the night and bends, transmits and absorbs the light around me. There is no escape. I feel the strain of my journey, a map of terror and estrangement I must surely, by now, wear well.

Kad and I are running through the streets, dodging the light cast in between as much as possible. Our feet splash over puddles of black tar. I don't bother to blink. My eyes are burning on the vista, my brain melted and rotted to mulch in my skull.

There seem to be no more deranged animals screaming at the sky - in fact, the night is so quiet and black that it hums. I catch a reflection of Kad and me at a wide angle, distorted in the black ponds. Our quantum bodies are on the run here but could be convulsing in a laboratory cage somewhere else.

No.

That's Dunwoody talking.

I have no idea where we're going. I just follow. I'm good at following it appears. A vision of the kid's oozing veil makes me shudder.

Kad makes a sharp turn into the aluminium glass pavilion of the old PLATO'S GATE motel. The front entrance to the building swings open with a mechanical screech. Everyone in the lobby is dead or having spasms like capsized turtles.

'I already inserted my own data into the hotels biometric security system. Before we do anything, we'll have to take a retinal scan and that'll give you admission to the bridal suite. If you try and enter the room without permitted access, then the alarm system will sound and our cover will be blown.'

'Okay, you lead the way.'

47

We head to an elevator ceilinged with a crystalline honeycomb of mirrored panels. The light reflects and refracts our bodies like a giant kaleidoscope. We catch our breath. Look at each other and communicate initially through relieved smiles.

'I thought I'd never see you again.' – I eventually let out. She touches the side of my cheek and grazes me with her elongated fingernails. I feel a sensation of static electricity bind us in its charge. She smells of lemongrass and old books. My shadow-shrouded doppelganger looks on greedily from behind his blanket.

'You should be so lucky.'

'Listen, I got this.' – I hand Kad the brass glove that Ursula the witch gave me back in the alleyway. A paroxysm of laughter escapes from her that seems inappropriately timed. I see a harvest moon, burning orange, come into view above the transmission tower.

Is Kad just a tactile illusion? Wouldn't that be just my luck?

'It's almost convenient you'd find something like that. You always were good at coming across good luck.'

- I was?

'I guess the biggest stroke of luck I had was finding you. At least with this glove I can keep up with you now.'- Kad looks embarrassed but forces a grateful smile. Her jaw clenches in the wake of receiving my compliment.

'No hard feelings about throwing you out?' – She asks.

'Huh? No, none at all. None. I understand.'

'Well, I guess I felt bad or something, that's why I came back for you. Turns out the Aerial Hotel had an escape chute all along.'

'Really?'

'Yeah, the evacuation slide took me right down to the foundation level of the building. That's how the zombie got in, he tore through the fabric. Had to fight a whole bunch of them off in the end and make my way back through the city streets. We would've been sitting ducks in that place, I guess we got lucky. Anyway, you didn't leave the hatchway open. I wanted to tell you and…apologise.' – This isn't easy for her. It's quite something to have to admit such a mistake when survival is so dependent on complete self-belief.

'Forget about it.' – I feel the weight of indignity and guilt lift from my shoulders. The elevator pings and the access opens to a floor of seemingly infinite doors.

'Come on, I'm hiding out in the bridal suite. The People haven't bothered me there so far. I think it's because the lights are busted.'

She leads me through the halls and stops at a door numbered 295.

'This is it.'

Kad leans into the biometric device and a beam of blue light scans the length of her left iris. The metal profile cylinder clicks, and the door opens. I do the same and am relieved to hear the cylinder click in acceptance. Inside the bridal suite there are four planks of wood zigzagged across the French doors. The mirrors all have a riveted, antique silver frame.

Kad is right, all the light has been gobbled up by shadow.

'I know we're hardly honeymooners but at least it's halfway classy. No hatchways or escape chutes to worry about.'

- I wish…wish we were honeymooners.

'It's perfect.'

'Glad you like it.'

I grab the hook of her arm and turn her towards me. She panics, I can tell she thinks I'm going to kiss her. *But...*

'Kad…do you ever dream?' – I ask, not even sure why.

'What kind of question is that?'

'A perfectly reasonable one I thought.'

Kad takes a moment. At first, I think she's chosen to dismiss the question entirely. But then she looks at me with an earnest expression.

'Nowadays I dream of nothing. I remember before, I dreamt about…acid.'

'Acid?'

- Better than dreaming of fucking mirrors constantly.

'All the time, like a recurring nightmare. I dreamt about being forced to take an acid bath by these guys in lab coats. I dream of my body being stuffed into a 40-gallon drum and having concentrated sulphuric acid or Sodium hydroxide poured over me. By the end, I'm only identifiable by my gallstone and dentures. I wake up screaming and nursing these phantom chemical burns' - Kad sits on the edge of the elegant four-post bed, rubs her knuckles a little self-consciously.

'Scientists?'

Kad looks at me and gives a convicting smirk.

'Unbelievable.'

'What?' – I ask all defensive.

'You're buying into Dunwoody's bullshit.'

'I'm not!'

- I totally am.

'You are…'

- I am.

'I'm not! All I'm saying is that you can't prove either way, really. Can you? I like to think of myself as agnostic on the subject.'

'Jesus…Hell is empty.' - For some people imagination is the greatest weapon against reality, Kad finds denial much more effective.

'I *want* to dream of a young boy, me, before I became a man, curled up by the inglenook. Stars bursting in the sky like scintillas of light.'

'This isn't a poem. Life isn't a poem.' – she snarls. Her eyes bleed through the cosy penumbra like chatoyant jewels.

'Maybe if I describe it in a poetic enough way then life *will* become a poem?'

'I sincerely doubt that.'

- Ouch.

'How do you explain the people vomiting black tar? How do you explain Dunwoody's demonic possession of that kid? And your dreams about the guys in lab-coats? Why can't I remember my own fucking name? Why do you think you can't remember…?'

'Hey, I remember just fine. And your name is Kurt.'

'Kurt? I don't…I'm not sure that that *is* my name.'

'Sure it is. You were wearing a nametag when we first met.'

'I was?'

'Jesus, you don't remember?'

- NO!

'Um…no, I don't.'

'So what do *you* dream of?'

- Ha! Here we go. Good luck not sounding crazy here Kurtis.

I take a deep breath, try to fix the words in my head and arrange them into speech.

'I think I dream of mirrors. Every night. Then I wake up and all I see is my forlorn reflection mirrored at me from this shimmering city. It's like I'm being forced to evaluate my own appearance with every waking moment - browbeaten into introspection. The only other option would be to cut out my own eyes or just fucking kill myself. That said, even with my constant image projected back at me all the time, I still don't think I have any definable characteristics.'

- *Fucking mirrors.*

'Well…you're handsome and rather pathetic.'

- *Pathetic, great.*

'Thank you.'

Kad looks at me fondly, maybe for the first time in our relationship.

A noise comes from the bathroom of the bridal suite. Panic shoots through me instantly and I throw myself against the back wall. I see Kad grin, amused by the reaction.

'Still skittish as ever I see?'

'What's that noise? You *did* hear that?'

A woman appears in the doorway, dark skinned, mid-thirties with hair wound into ringlets. It occurs to me straightaway that she is *very* beautiful, glamourous even, and there is an elicited lurching in my loins that feels profound and unfamiliar.

'This is Ailsa. We met just after I evacuated the Aerial Hotel. An ex-writer I believe? She's a dark dweller like us. Thinks Miles Dunwoody is the living incarnation of evil. She can handle herself too.'

I extend a greeting to Ailsa and she meets me with a firm clasp that cracks the bone around my hand, the good hand.

'Pleased to meet you...?' - Ailsa's cockiness sticks in my chest, dissolves into an angry warm resentment and dribbles down to my belly.

'Kurt…I *think*?'

'You *think*?' – she bulges her big cartoon eyes out at me.

'We're still kind of unclear about the specifics of my identity.'

- That sounds ridiculous. I sound ridiculous.

Ailsa raises her eyebrows and takes a seat next to Kad on the four-post bed.

'Good to have you on board. I like the hand-gear.' – Ailsa motions to the brass claw.

'A witch called Ursula gave it to me.'

- Talk about witches. That'll make you seem less ridiculous.

'A witch huh? Sometimes I think we have bigger nutjobs to worry about than Dunwoody.'

I offer Ailsa a smile, but her dismissiveness bothers me. How does she know witchcraft is such nonsense? Is it any dumber than how we've chosen to live our lives? Not just this, but seeing Ursula as a child of the light, consuming the flesh of her cynics still sits on the edge of my gut like a sick dog with worms.

'I'm sure glad I stumbled across *this* little firecracker.' – She says, addressing Kad and nudging her in the shoulder.

- Wait…firecracker?

'What?'

'*What*? What did I say?'

'What did you just call her?'

53

'I dunno…a firecracker? Guess I've been listening to The People too much, but hey, haven't we all? She is though. This girl is ballsy and mean as fuck. Those insects don't stand a chance.' – She bats her artificially long eyelashes.

- *What's this talk about insects suddenly? This girl bears watching. Not just because she's gorgeous.*

'Right…no argument there.'

My sexual awakening changes to abject confusion. This doesn't fit. There's something about Ailsa, something artificial.

I mean, she's wearing an immaculately pressed high waistline crop top that exposes a laminate of stiff abs, hardly suitable post-apocalypse attire if you ask me.

Camouflage leggings too? Moisturized and perfumed. This girl looks ready for a night on the fucking tiles, hardly a writer or a fighter. She certainly doesn't appear to have seen the same horrors Kad and I have lay witness to. If she had she wouldn't be so fucking upbeat.

- *Her happiness isn't real.*

Ailsa reminds me of the scantily clad femme fetale you'd find in a male-chauvinist melodrama about the walking dead. She isn't realistic. I just, I don't know – I just don't trust her physical form at all. In fact, I would ridicule her creator for their lack of imagination.

But for now, with Kad's contentment resting on Ailsa and me getting on, I'll reserve my judgement.

I look at Kad and meet her gaze, a gaze that holds our universe together. I wish she knew she inspired my dreams so.

- *Go on. Tell her.*

'You know Dunwoody says you're just a cat brain wired to a reality simulator?'

'He mentioned me? By name?'

'He did.'

'Wow. I can't believe he knows my name.' – Kad almost…*blushes*.

'You sound more than a little flattered by this acknowledgment. You like that he notices you?'

She scoffs, juts her head back in a gesture of disregard.

'No way. He represents everything I hate about men. I'm just, I dunno, surprised I guess.'

'Is that so?'

- You're in love with him you bitch.

The room goes quiet and we are left in the kind of silence only humans can create – a human silence, with tense breathing and squirming scalps and fabric pressing against the angles of our flesh-buried bones. Outside, screams play like bum notes from a blind musician.

'There's always tomorrow. A new day. There are no mistakes waiting for us tomorrow.'

- Just the aftermath of the mistakes we create in the present.

Chris Kelso

RULES OF THE PEOPLE

THREE

The People place restrictions on the quartering of soldiers in private homes without the owner's consent, prohibiting it during peacetime.

Chris Kelso

Five -

Ailsa has fallen asleep peacefully coiled up in a ball on the floor. She reminds me of a family pet from another life. Maybe I was the family pet?

Kad approaches me with an empty rucksack in her hand. Her look is of confounded irritation.

'You don't seriously believe all this BS about us being animals hooked up to a computer, do you? What a load of baloney!'

'I'm not saying I believe it, I'm just saying…what if?'

'We can't afford to have 'what ifs'! That's when the day seekers get you and Dunwoody brainwashes you into thinking he's Harry Krishna!' – She regulates the volume of her voice to a disgruntled whisper for the sake of the slumbering Ailsa. I do the same.

'That won't happen, trust me…'

'You told me once when we were drunk one time, back at the Aerial Hotel, that you didn't trust your own willpower. You called *yourself* "weak-minded".'

'Well, hey, maybe I'm a retarded farm animal! Maybe I've been pumped full of drugs and hormones. Maybe that's why I'm weak-minded!'

- Maybe…

Kad sighs and makes for the door. On the way out, she says she's hitting the supply stores for provisions. I call after her, tell her I'll come help her loot, but she ignores me and closes the door with a thump. Good job 'Kurt'…

Our balcony view would've been of the council building across the road - a geodesic dome made of tempered glass. Dunwoody's face leers out from it and from behind the curtain walls of each skyscraper. Ailsa untangles herself from her ball on the floor like an onyx Adder. She stretches her arms out while yawning.

'Kind of vicious, weren't you?' – She says, wiping the grog from the corners of her eyes. I notice a bruise around her neck, like rope burns.

'Vicious?'

I can't believe how good she looks. My hunger returns. Before I know it, I have her pinned against the wall of the bridal suite, my fingers clutched around her tiny, slender shoulders with far too much vigour. The brute rises from within. *What the fuck am I doing?*

'I'll show you vicious…'

'Oh yeah.'

'Yeah!'

A sexual force pulsates through me like electricity, something that has haunted my internal devices for what feels like an age, jacking my heart and stirring the fluid in my gut to a boiling frenzy. I feel the hard dick shrink my underwear. I need her. I've been bitten by the vampire of lust. I throw her to the floor. Ailsa is as light and fragile as I imagined her to be. She lets me exert myself, stabs me with a stiff tongue—my first kiss.

She begs me to choke her, to throttle her hard until she starts making a wheezing sound and her eyeballs rinse white and she climaxes without any need for penetration.

'Choke me! Choke me!'

I tell Ailsa to get on all fours – she obeys - and I start peeling her leggings down to the backs of her knees. I observe the fleshy knolls of her presented buttocks for a moment, marvelling and utterly possessed by arousal, before thrusting my face between the cleft. I lap at salt and battery acid-sharp sweat, enjoy the taste of her natural juices so much that I let out an involuntary snarl. I become even more aware of the strong, burning hard-on tucked tightly into my underwear and of its desire to be freed.

Then, I'm unbuckled and mounting the girl. I don't ask, I just take. The territoriality. The sheer sense of belonging. Of intimacy. Confidence swells in my skull. I feel awake and more cognisant than I ever have before.

Have I just this minute come online? I am aware of being judged by my lower dimensions. A paranoid thought whirrs through my mind and takes up a fixed residence with schizophrenic passion.

My penis.

Does it make the grade?

Eventually the thought scatters when lust takes complete control.

It feels like the first time.

***

I had not intended to use Ailsa in this way, as an object for such intense carnal perversions, but here I am. Cupid paints blind I suppose. I suppose.

Her eyes are not deep, yet they hold me like a speck of light in a sunbeam. Ailsa's irises reflect back at me when we have sex. I feel like I'm fucking myself into the abyss. I have to hand it to the girl though - she picked up the shattered pieces of me and tried her best to give them back to me in the correct order. But I am an impossible puzzle.

'We can't do this again.' – I say this after disgorging. If it's any consolation, I feel like a complete asshole.

'Why?'

'It's getting too serious already. I don't want that for you.'

'Is this serious?'

'Yes!'

'You don't want anything serious?'

'What does that even mean? Serious?'

- You know what serious means in this context you prick.

She sighs, but her sigh is a question I cannot answer. Ailsa roles off me.

'Kurt, I've given you all and now I am nothing.'

'I'm sorry, Ailsa.'

She embraces me again, this ruined man-thing. I've looked at this face too long now, seen too many mirrors, dreamt too often of smashing my body into a million jagged shards. I embrace Ailsa back. And I embrace her airbrushed perfectness.

I want to ask about the bruise around her neck but get a sense that, if she did try to unsuccessfully kill herself once before, then she made the decision to do so on her own and no amount of talking about it would change her mind if she took the notion to try again.

Her features are as perfect and symmetrical as the city. Together it works; we are both seeking something we can't otherwise obtain. I could never love this girl though. Fucking her only made me realise that my heart belongs to another.

She pulls her head up to look at me with those dead spherical fish eyes, her make-up still flawless.

'You should know something.'

'Mm?' – I ask, buckling up my trousers and heaving my body from the crime scene floor.

'I know you're not a real person, fake somehow.'

'Excuse me?'

- Fuck. She knows…

'It's okay. I still feel the same for you. I can just…tell you're not human. The way you feel, inside and out, it's not natural. You have shallowness to you. Like one of the insects, like the arachnids.'

Ailsa's indictment catches me off guard. *'Unnatural', 'fake', 'shallow'* - these are exactly the same adjectives I'd use to describe *her*!

'You think *I'm* fake and shallow?'

'Well…yeah. I'm not trying to upset you, I'm just being honest, and I hope you believe me when I say I like those aspects of who you are. I'm shallow and fake too. We work well.'

She was right.

'Don't worry. I know you can't love me, you're not capable. I couldn't love anything more than my daughter or my ex-husband anyway.'

'Where are they?'

'They're…somewhere else entirely.'

The pristine white of the nameless conglomerate buildings burns through the plywood-girded French doors of the bridal suite. I must admit, the light continues to compel me.

'I think I'm going to die here Ailsa.'

'Me too. Manhattan was supposed to be my quiet place to die. I was meant to die there.'

'Why Manhattan?'

'Fuck knows. I meet people like me all the time. People just looking for a quiet place to die. Whoever suggested Manhattan was out of their fucking mind.'

- It must be better than this place, honey.

Ailsa and I get clothed and tidy up the place a little for Kad's return. She bursts back in, all out of breath and bloodied, just as I tuck my shirt into my waistline. I feel a new layer of sweat gloss my forehead and down my back – so this is what the fear of almost getting caught is like?

What a rush.

'What happened?' – Ailsa asks, masking her flushed, just-fucked face with expert ease. Kad takes a moment to regain a steadier breathing pattern. I'm paranoid the hotel room smells like forbidden sex.

'The zombies…The People, they're fucking everywhere. Even the witches, the other factions, they're all converted. I got chased back to the hotel. I'm sure I lost 'em.'

'Least you're alright.' - Ailsa possesses a kind of blithe nonchalance that I just can't relate to.

Kad lost her rucksack during the escape. Ailsa and I go in to wrap our arms around her to comfort, but she backs away from both of us like we've got the plague.

Does she know what happened between us? Can she smell the brine of illicit fucking?

Is she angry?

Why would she be?

There's been no indication Kad has any romantic inclinations towards me whatsoever. It might hurt my chances if I ever want to declare any feelings for her down the line. I wouldn't worry about that. I don't have the balls to express myself anyway…

Chris Kelso

Ailsa

Spiders are everywhere, roaming. Everywhere. Kurt…

This city is teeming with them. It's gotten so I can't turn a corner or pass someone on the street without coming face to face with one of the bastards. They look and act like us, assume the forms of people we know and love. Underneath though, well, that's a different story.

Before you know what's what they're shitting webs out their asses and scaling the condominiums to report back to their superiors. When I get home, they're hiding under my couch, conducting reconnaissance missions across my kitchen counter.

The laundry room outside my apartment building is infested! You can't just give them a wide berth because they're fucking everywhere.

I told myself Kurt, I said *this* will be my last novel, my 'drunk' novel. I feel like I'm soberer drunk than when I haven't touched a drop. Things seem *so* much clearer after a few. I realise that, soberly, I have NOTHING to say. Nothing new, certainly.

At least drunkenly I can channel some form of genuine, authentic emotion into writing – even if it is just drunken gibberish. My sober novels are awful. My sober novels make my own children disappear. Maybe my drunken ones will be better.

They couldn't be any worse surely?

I'm going to tell you about me, Ailsa Atkins – a distinctly unremarkable person. An underachiever, broken-hearted wanderer of a lonely, indifferent town in a cultureless landscape.

This is my life. I have always made bad decisions. I know there is nothing new here, but if we probe a little, maybe...?

In Manhattan, my daughter and I drive across the East River with no particular destination in mind. That's how I know Dunwoody isn't a prophet, that's how I know he's lying about where we came from. I was a person once. Not an animal.

The Manhattan Bridge swaying over the great gulf of water and I'm sure my 10-year-old daughter and I both fantasised about the suspension wires snapping and us both being swallowed up by the great black gorge.

So, I pull the car over. We get out, head to the footpath and brood into the East River. A jogger hurtles by. He's wearing earphones and listening to alien mind control transmissions.

The view is beautiful. Most people prefer the Brooklyn Bridge but not me, although maybe I'm biased. There are no sad reflective memories associated with the Manhattan side.

My husband and I used to walk the Brooklyn Bridge at Sunset, and then head to the Promenade, down Montague Street in Brooklyn Heights. This is a long time ago, before my daughter came along and long before I started fantasizing about this glass city. Before the spiders.

I ask if she's okay. She shrugs, reaches across to scratch her shoulder.

'I said, you okay kiddo?'

Another shrug.

'I'm okay.'

I remember that my daughter had been moodier than usual lately. They say 10 is a difficult age for a girl, we used to dread her 13th birthday. It might also have something to do with the fact that my husband, her father, left us for a chief inspector and covert agent a few months before. His new girlfriend has since converted him. They live together in the Lincoln Tower on the Upper West Side. I haven't seen them since I came to this city.

Despite the fact his allegiances have turned I still love him, and, I know it's terrible to say it, but my daughter was the tenuous link between my ex-husband and I. Occasionally we met in passing and exchange perfunctory greetings, pretending to have moved on with our lives.

But how could I be over that? I love him.

'Do you know about the Slave State?'

I ask her, referring to a lame book I read in high school. She shakes her head – no.

'You know how mother writes books?'

She nods – *uh, huh*.

'Well, that's what she writes about. Stuff like the Slave State.'

Having never previously showed an interest in my books or their content, I knew this might be a hard sell. My daughter wasn't interested in anything - except video games and, probably, a strong subconscious desire to die which she probably inherited from her old mother.

Spiders are everywhere and I'm talking to a 10-year-old about the Slave State.

The Staten Island ferry chugs into view and no one on board looks bothered by the arachnid onslaught.

'You see all this around you? The big buildings and the cluster of humanity? Well, it's bullshit baby.'

'I know.'

The statement takes me off guard.

'You do?'

She nods.

'What're your theories?'

She shrugs – 'I don't have any theories. I just always knew it was bullshit.'

We wait in silence a moment as a cyclist whizzes past, as if he might be a spy listening in to our conversation. He disappears down the footpath towards the gleaming metal chopsticks of the Manhattan skyline.

A megadose of adrenaline is surging through my brain and body – even just recollecting it makes me relive the feeling. For the first time in my entire relationship with my daughter I feel like we are connecting. I don't probe her any further about the Slave State, it's enough that she is sceptical.

She'll come to the reality of things on her own terms. I feel a surge of something else. It could be pride. I made this kid and he's as beautifully aware of himself and his environment as any hardened conspiracy theorist. I remember thinking, *this* is the future of humanity. *This* kid right here, *my* kid. I reach out to put my hand on her shoulder, but I remember something…I remember I never had a daughter.

I'm not a writer either, never was. I was a model and a skateboarder. I was at Mount Trashmore, one of only three women boarding professionally at the time.

I feel the hope fade away as my waking dream dissipates. I fill up with a nasty energy. The nasty energy has never left me. I wonder if my husband is still with the chief inspector Slave State agent…I start wondering if I'm even on the Manhattan Bridge.

So, what's next? – I thought. What's the *next* daydream? Did I ever have a daughter?

I look back at my car. The concave façade of the skyscrapers has focused a spotlight of sunshine on it and melted the wing mirrors. The tyres have been burst and the bonnet is jacked open. Someone has been checking the engine.

Another jogger speeds past. This was the first time I heard the spiders scuttling. Now they're back. You can only outrun them for so long…

So, I climb over the steel railings, loud subway trains rumble by on four different tracks overhead. I'm compelled to explore the guts of the bridge.

The sea is roaring below, the residue of my ghost daughter still palmed across my brain and internal structures like sodium cyanide. I try to shake it off. The Black Dog bursts free from its kennel, scales the barbed wire mesh of the holding pen and bolts with ferocious intent down the streets, darkness trailing in its wake. I see the skyline fall beneath a shadow.

On the underpass, I hear a noise coming from above me. Rats scratching around in the girders. Spiders conglomerating. My eyes follow the steel planks and I locate the source of the scratching. It seems someone has constructed a base between the girders using wood, probably discarded materials from nearby Chinatown.

I climb up the rail and carefully lift the cardboard trap door. The base is roughly ten feet-by-one-and-a-half feet and protected with bike locks. A make-shift hideout from the coming invasion, shelter from the spiders, Dunwoody and the starving blackness.

The city is about to be overrun by mongrels and insects. The hallucinations are only the beginning.

I remember tearing up the wood and pulling down the previous tenant's belongings, including pots, bedsheets, clothing and even electrical items. I don't know who lived there before I came along, but I concluded that I was evicting them. It's a Black Dog eats Black Dog world out there.

I'll hide out here – I thought. I'll write myself a new reality. I've read so much about the Slave State that it started penetrating my consciousness. Then I woke up here.

I'm sick of this plague. The Black Dog was always bound to come back, get its revenge. Hell - *revenge* implies that the last time it fought humanity it lost. It didn't lose. It can't lose.

You certainly can't win.

You just can't win…

What must the world be like for a man who has never loved himself or felt the love of another? It must taste a little like waking up in this place every day…

<u>Six</u> -

'Throw ink at paper. Hope for pattern to emerge…'
- Jay McInerney

I wake up before Kad on the four-post bed. She's spread-eagled across my legs, so when I go to move I wind up stirring her into consciousness with me. Kad growls under her breath at being woken prematurely.

I look around for Ailsa. Not in the living room. No sign of her in the kitchenette. Not in the bathroom or out in the lobby.

My cock is still half-stiff at the thought of her one-dimensionality. I'm convinced her soul scraped stare will never leave me.

'Where's Ailsa?' - I ask Kad who is still a little bleary but fully pissed off.

'I don't know. Maybe she went out or something.'

'*Out*? Without saying anything to either of us?'

'I told you I don't know.' - Kad gets up grumbling, sweeps aside the fringe of her lank black hair. We've fallen asleep side by side before - I often enjoy the faint tickle of her wandering strands on the back of my neck like wild filopodia.

- Jesus, I've got it bad.

I see, pinned to the intersected plywood over the window, a wad of scratchpad paper with a note written on. From Ailsa –

-

Dear Kurt and Kad,

I'm sorry to leave you both so suddenly. I'm going to find my daughter and my ex-husband. I know I can get back to them somehow. My experience with both of you has been a kind of affirmation for me, that there is still love and pleasure to be had in the world. Thank you, both of you.

But there is really only one person who can help me find my estranged family again – Miles Dunwoody.

This may seem like a sudden change in attitude, but I can't explain it. I truly hope you don't hate me for it. Kad, being with you for a few days made me realise that resilience is key to survival. You remind me of my daughter. You're so strong and determined, but tender, smart and funny too.

I think you guys would both get along famously. You're the type of woman I want to be. Even though you do have a weakness for men that're bad for you, I can't even think how many times you've saved my ass, I know Kurt feels the same about you.

We both owe you our lives. That's why I have to be honest with you. I respect you too much to have you believe I was something I'm not. The truth is, I haven't really seen much of the street-level action, I only recall being out on the Schism for a couple of hours before you picked me up and brought me to PLATO'S GATE. I never killed a zombie in my life. I never had to scavenge or use any initiative.

I don't hate Dunwoody either. In fact, I think I love him. I know this must disgust you after everything I told you before. I love him in the way a Christian loves God or a Muslim loves al-Ala. I want to worship him. He neither begets nor is born, nor is there to Him, in my opinion, any equivalent. I have somehow absorbed your dreams of acid baths, I hope you don't mind. I feel like they keep me pure and honest.

Kurt – you remind me so much of my husband. He too was a shallow, lost person. I don't say this to upset you, I love my husband very much. I also like you a lot. You are handsome and, I think, harmless. My whole life I've fought the state, tried to write something that was new or original or cutting edge.

Now I'm just tired of all the constant fighting. I'm not a very convincing character, am I? I know you can see through me, through this phony veneer I've created for myself.

I never understood Invasion of the Body Snatchers as a concept. I get the whole 'need to survive' part, but the alien seedpods arrived on earth and wanted to survive too, they required our bodies to endure.

Classic human beings - instead of accepting this as the next stage of evolution, by saving an alien race and co-habiting peacefully with them, we're expected to fight for this grand sense of human-ness?

It made sense for the humans to accept the parasite into their systems, to relinquish their autonomy, the ambition and excitement and the stresses that come with those things. I mean, the human remains basically the same, right?

All you're really doing is sacrificing the worst parts of yourself. It would effectively save the planet - we could no longer reproduce and destroy rainforests. And we're no better than they are, I mean we've wiped out indigenous populations and ruined ecosystems in the name of survival, haven't we? And we couldn't even let go of that? Isn't that insanely petty and selfish?

The nature of the beast.

I'd have embraced the pod-people. I wish there was a body snatcher treatment where you fall asleep next to a pod and the spores get to work duplicating you exactly so we all fit in – kind of like multicellular communism.

The pods can replicate your precise atomic value, we could absorb the spore as easily as static electricity. You'd all be like me, dead like the moon.

Anyway, I appreciate what you both did for me and to thank you I've decided not to turn you in to Dunwoody straight away. But at some stage, in the next couple of days, we will, I'm sure, be making an appearance at the PLATO'S GATE hotel.

Yours

Ailsa the Allmaziful, the everliving, the bringer of plurabilities, haloed be her eve, her singtime sung, her rill be run, unhemmed as it is uneven.

The world had changed...along with it he had changed. As the colour leached from the planet, indeed the entire world, it was replaced with disease. Now there was little to do but nurture that disease like a hungry child. It was the only thing left. It was all that mattered now.

***

'Ailsa the Allmaziful, the Everliving, the Bringer of Plurabilities, haloed be her eve, her singtime sung, her rill be run, unhemmed as it is uneven!'

'What does *that* mean?' – I say this as I crumple up the letter in my fist and throw it onto the floor of the bridal suite. We're so used to the screams they're starting to sound like maidens singing in a choir. Kad searches the cloud of names and finds the answer.

'It's from Finnegan's Wake. I think it's something to do with how universally loved Miles Dunwoody is. Pretty abstract and opaque.'

'Universal implies there is something else out there. There is only here, only this city.'

- You're being much too negative. Don't drag her down with you.

'Kurt, I'm going to show you. I'm going to prove to you that there is something outside the city's strictures.' - Her optimism is kind of invigorating, like a dream of halcyon days gone by.

- I could kiss you.

Kad is trying her best to keep my spirits high. Don't get me wrong, I appreciate her efforts, I appreciate that she cares, but I can feel myself overcome by a new force.

A dramatic shift in priorities has arisen. I feel like I need to articulate myself sexually. Ailsa has infected me with hunger. Let me tell you, I'm fucking famished already. It takes all my effort not to attack Kad. She turns to me, as if sensing the rapid adjustment in my personality.

'I should tell you that…Ailsa and I…we were…together.' – She says almost regretfully.

– *Fuck…*

'You mean you…?'

'Yeah. I have no idea how it happened. I mean I'm not…I've never been…you know?'

'Into other girls?'

'Well exactly. There was something about her. Something parasitic…I don't mean that to sound offensive. I like Ailsa, a lot.' – She rubs the jagged corner of her left wrist, nervously adjusts the bangle on the right.

I can't shake the image of Kad and Ailsa in romantic union. What's this? The first impulse towards pornography? The dormant itch of Neanderthal pursuit? I'm a small man, pale and suffering. Can't you at least give me *something*?

'She and I also had a brief tryst.'

'You did? Huh…'

- I don't think she believes me.

'Yeah, I don't know where it came from either. Initially I felt like I had forced myself on her, then it occurred to me that she totally orchestrated the whole thing. Like, yes, like a parasite. She used us.'

Kad and I sit there in awkward stillness for a few long seconds. I wonder if she really believes Ailsa and I slept together. Why do I care so much?

- Oh – yeah, because I'm in love with Kad and the thought of making her jealous fills me with a strange and ugly satisfaction.

'We need more supplies but there's no way to get out onto the streets safely to loot. Ailsa and I used all the provisions I took from the Aerial Hotel.'

'Aren't you forgetting where we are?'

'How'd you mean?' – She asks.

'This is a hotel! The PLATOS GATE hotel! We have over 80 floors of rooms with full minibar privilege!'

'What if The People are there waiting for us? At least in room 295 we know we're safe.'

'For now, yes, but we need food and drink. There's more chance of us surviving in here than out there on The Schism.'

Kad waits a beat, considers our options.

'I guess you're right.'

- *Well, there's a first time for everything!*

In the mirror, my glacial pond
Narcissus thaws
And the future becomes present
To me
A witch and her coven, I see
1, 2, 3
Conducting a spell in the alleyway
Of a primeval city
And then
+10
Joy escapes me,
As I feed on the misery caught up in the atmosphere
While all my love
Sits suspended in a piled-hotel
If there was any justice
If I had any control
I'd make them cast a spell on her

Easy as 2, 9, 5
To finally see me as a man
And not as a burden

Chris Kelso

Plato's Gate –

'Real nobility is based on scorn, courage, and profound indifference.'
- Albert Camus

We take a floor each – Kad is checking the apartments neighbouring room 295, I take the service elevator to the level above. In the mirrored box I replay my encounter with Ailsa. I imagine how much better it would be with Kad.

- Clear your head man! There's work to do! This is about survival not reproduction!

The elevator pings and the access parts to a vast, empty corridor of numbered rooms. I try the first door I come to but have to double take.

Room 295?

But, how can that be? I almost turn back but remember that our need is great and Kad is depending on me. The visual biometric device has been disabled, torn out, exposing its circuit board. The lock is already busted and I can push it open with a light shove.

A room, virtually identical to the bridal suite, complete with four-post bed and plywood shielded window, is revealed. I cross the threshold and the feeling of Deja-Vu is so obvious and moving that I'm nearly embarrassed to even mention it.

A toilet flushes and the bathroom door opens. I raise my brass claw to head level, pointing the spikes downward ready to defend myself. Part of me half expects Ailsa to walk out, like I'm stuck in some temporal

85

loop and I'm just wandering the space-time on a repeat setting.

A lanky man wearing a yellow sports top and tracksuit bottoms appears and leans on the doorway. He has cropped blonde hair and an indifferent face. Why is everyone who isn't part of The People such an aloof sociopath?

- Look in the mirror, friend.

I'm beginning to wonder.

- Anyway, who says he's not with The People?

'Who're you?' – He asks in a foreign accent. He doesn't look in the least bit intimidated by my serrated glove.

'I'm Kurt. Who're you?'

'I'm Henrik.' – he booms.

'Are you…?'

He laughs. It booms also.

'One of the People? No, but I doubt I'd tell you even if I was.'

'Aren't you going to ask me if I'm a Dunwoody sympathiser?'

'Nah. I know you're not. You don't look the type. There's no hope left in your eyes.'

'Well, doesn't everyone know me *so* well?'

'Must be great being so predictable. You alone?'

'No…I…I have a friend. She's checking the rest of the hotel for supplies.'

'No point. I got 'em all.' – He says glibly.

'You got *all* the supplies in this entire hotel?'

'Yeah, I got 'em all.'

- Fuck off…

'I've been here for a very long time, Johnny.'

'It's Kurt.'

'Okay, listen Johnny, you look like a nice guy. How about you let me tag along with you and your partner in exchange for some of my supplies?'

'Where exactly are your supplies stored?'

'I got them hidden in various nooks and crannies throughout the rooms on this floor.'

'What makes you so sure I won't just try and kill you and take them?'

Henrik simpers smugly and rolls his eyes.

'You don't look the type. Trust me, I know.'

'I've killed people out on The Schism.' – I lie.

- Fuck sake, NO ONE is buying that!

Henrik looks at me and detaches himself from the doorway portal.

'Come in here. I need to show you something.'

I follow Henrik into the bathroom, my brass-claws clenched and prepared for attack. The smell of rotten flesh and sulphuric acid attacks my senses.

- What the…?

I'm faced with Henrik's giant, broad-backed shoulders. He moves aside and exposes a girl's body in an early state of putrefaction.

She looks remarkably like Kad, but Henrik assures me her name is Anja Holmström. The girl has been disembowelled and tampered with, her organs spill out like dropped chow mein.

Her left hand has four missing fingers, just like mine. I feel nauseous. For some reason I don't just turn around and tear Henrik's murderous face off with one swipe of my right hand.

He sits on the edge of the bath as if he's about to tell

me who he really is. Captain Nemo meets Jack the Ripper.

I sit on the toilet seat and prepare to listen. Everyone has a story but me...

I relinquish myself to the significance of a single three digit number.

Henrik

- Oh Kurt. It was 1994; I didn't know what the fuck I was doing half the time. The People would never have approved.

Everyone was so caught up in the Swedish national teams triumphant bronze medal win in the USA I think, I'm sure, a nuclear bomb could've hit the town of Ryd, Linkoping, and no one would've averted their gaze.

I'm not like *you* people, not at all. I'm not human. You think the People would ever have an alien as a member?

You can find Linkoping on a map, we're buried in the regions of Östergötland - 'Land of the Eastern Geats' in English - Geats being one of the two primary groups that merged into what we now know as contemporary Swedes (sort of like what the Anglo-Saxons are to the present day English I suppose).

Honest, I'd never killed another person before Billy Ackerman, The People don't believe in murder for murders sake. I think there is one loophole in the Rules that permit killing, for the life of me I can't remember what it is.

So you can only imagine what must've been going through my adolescent mind when Anders Nilsson, the most popular kid in ninth grade, asked me to murder Billy Akerman, probably the most *un*-popular kid in the year below, in exchange for a bag of beautiful clay cat's-eye marbles – right?

Nilsson must've seen the potential in me though, caught sight of the ugly spirit resting dormant behind my stare. He selected *me* specifically, he did. You people are as

89

quietly devious and manipulative as you are violent. But anyway...

It became common knowledge that I *did* kill a cat once - ate from its brain and took a primal cut from its rump. But that was about the sum total of my homicidal behaviour prior to my thirteenth birthday.

My paediatrician, a child-molester in a double vented jacket, seemed more pissed off that I'd risked getting Creutzfeldt-Jakob disease from the infectious proteins in the cat's brain.

It's weird, nothing much came from killing that cat. Billy Akerman was different, of course, from the cat I mean – although to this day I'm not sure I completely understand the massive distinction.

Around this time, a troupe of birds started watching me eat, fuck, they *still* follow me around. Some people get spiders, some get other insects. I get birds. Big ugly fuckin birds. They'd gather on the trees and just fucking leer at me, white as almond blossoms, as if they knew *something*. Outside—a staccato of fireworks.

Don't feel bad for Anja Holmström. Her father is Miles Dunwoody's biggest fan. This is another experiment. The second person I have killed, nine years after my first.

I can remember Anders Nilsson sitting at the apex of the jungle gym so clearly man, all bathed in natural light, like I had been summoned to the steps of an ancient temple to bow before some ancient solar deity.

Miles Dunwoody had nothing on this guy.

'I've got a proposition for you' – Akerman said with a grunt. His family were originally from Norrköping and people from Linkoping were a little intimidated by him. We were a university city, a hockey city. A bourgeoisie city. Ryd was a part of Linkoping full of students, or Muslim immigrants from Africa and the Middle East. People from Norrköping were a little more, what's the word…*blue-collar*. I guess I sound like a snob.

So Nilsson was leaning on his knees and jerked his neck to the left to hawk on the asphalt. He told me to join him atop the jungle-Jim. I did everything I was told man, climbed up to his perch like a good little bitch. Anders Nilsson wasn't the kind of kid you said no to in a hurry.

I heard he had been smoking cigarettes since he was, like, ten years old or something. To this day he is the only human being I have ever respected, even ephemerally.

Sitting there crouched beside this tough, out-of-town kid, I felt goddamned incredible - hoped Edit Klasson would see me socialising with the Nilsson boy (she didn't though, no one ever saw me when I wanted them to).

So he brought out the shiny orbs that seemed to hold entire galaxies within their cores. I looked at them (didn't touch them!), studied them in silent awe - the tinted crystal; ones with bands of fine glittering copper flakes injected into them; ones with strands of opaque white and coloured vanes streaked throughout the centre…fucking gorgeous. As marvellous as the architecture of this city. Have you seen the Aerial Hotel? It's stunning. These were more impressive. They all had this sort of iridescent finish. They looked valuable. They *were* valuable.

I told Nilsson I'd do whatever he wanted me to do, on the proviso that I could have these wondrous little marbles. It's amazing how kids prioritise, isn't it? Hey, I was *really* into marbles. They reminded me of my real home planet, wherever that was.

Billy Akerman was kind of a pain in the ass. He was short and fat and, by all accounts, an annoying little fucking spaz. No one really liked him all that much, but fucking Anders Nilsson hated him most of all man. Billy had this rare copy of 'Fantomen'. Anders claimed Billy stole the comic from him – I found out these claims were completely erroneous and Nilsson just wanted something else he didn't already have – or revenge on the person who was wealthier than he was. Course, Billy was already dead before I discovered this. I have never understood human beings.

Armed with a thumbscrew compass, I followed fat Billy Akerman home after school one afternoon. He always took a shortcut across the campus grounds – the porker was keen to get home to his grandmother's gross pickled herring dinners. I imagined inscribing a perfect arc in his skull.

I see Billy Ackerman's face on every mindless zombie I come across.

I remember too, it was trash day. Lines of refuse bins sat curbside, pregnant with garbage. I guess I liked this town, always have. Every lawn in Ryd is lush and always freshly-cut for summer.

Each house on my old avenue sat prettily opposite the verdant greens with their panels of white timber. I'd known most of my neighbours since I was a young kid, and liked most of them too. They were all real friendly folks and always assumed the best of people.

Outside my window were the sounds of the brawling water of Göta Kanal, the gentle idling of tourist boats, of happy people, inner calm, arsenic white sands on the horizon like a sudden stroke of snow on coloured canvas...

I took my compass out, splayed the legs apart like it were a switchblade and rammed the spike into the back of Billy Akerman's skull. It stuck hard in his fat head. It never ceases to amaze me how brittle and soft the human body is!

Why, Kurt, you know how fragile you are?

Billy started crying and yanked the protractor out, looking at the bloody needle point with pale horror. I told him to be quiet, at first quietly then with more aggression, and, I admit, I started getting cold feet then. I remembered the bag of awesome cat's-eye marbles and I punched him square in the nose, more with the limp of wrist than with my fist, but it made a satisfying *CRUNCH* and he fell to the floor like a bag of fucking cement. I don't know where the strength came from – fear and adrenaline maybe, I dunno. My father wasn't an athlete either, unless kicking the living shit out of my mother every night counted as a sport?

Birds gathered in a suspended configuration—the white cartel. I rolled Billy Akerman's body down an embankment and watched his body drift down river.

I know I'm not normal. It's not 'normal' to witness or commit unspeakable acts and be so impassive; to afford zero meaning to human life whatsoever. I *know* that's not normal. I'm trying to get a cure though, I'm looking for help - isn't that enough? That's what this Anja Holmström experiment is for, I'm trying to understand my sickness. Once I know what's missing, there'll be no more unnecessary death. I'm trying to do the right thing.

Whatever is missing from my moral centre, I want to

fill the void somehow. Is this how a modern god must feel? I could not shake the premonition. My god is a merciless god who hates all his creations equally. The dark throne above all those mountains of bone. A nitric bath awaits someone…

Something clings to my body like wet mud, it's not shame.

I met up with this guy called Leon Lifvendahl, an ethnic Swede from Skäggetorp. He agreed to meet me in the lobby of the Frimurarhotellet.

He was a skinny character with no eyebrows, stood about 7 feet tall and wore a white tracksuit with red racing stripes down each side. His skin was hard-looking and cracked all over the surface like a loose scab. Leon's eyes were guilt-stricken and soulless just like mine. Kind of like yours are too, Kurt.

Leon and I took the service elevator to the basement of the Frimurarhotellet. He promised me we were going to watch some snuff pornography. I wanted to see if I had any reaction to child murder as an adult. If it makes you feel any better, I really *wanted* to be sickened by it. Maybe I'll turn a corner someday. I want to hate myself for killing Billy and Anja. That's the whole point.

We walked through the ground floor parking level. The air smelled like linoleum and piss. Leon pulled out a bundle of master keys from his tracksuit pocket, located the correct fob and inserted it into the custodian janitor's closet door.

'Don't worry. The janitor knows we're here.' – Leon reassured me. The cam-lock clicked and the door swung open. I noticed that it was packed with junk, stacks of cardboard boxes full of god-knows-what. Leon flicked on the lights and a figure became half-illuminated sitting at a desk in the corner of the room.

'Esbjörn? It's Leon. I got a customer.'

The figure stood up slowly, inched out of his shadowy cape. Esbjörn the janitor was a heavy set man of about 50 with curly yellow hair, Norwegian descended you could tell. His face had kind, soft features. Nothing like mine.

He would be classic fodder for Dunwoody and his cronies.

'You got money?'

Leon butted in before I could talk.

'He's got an interest Esbjörn, a real interest….'

The Norwegian janitor and Leon shared a sinister smirk and I knew immediately what they'd concluded about me. They thought they'd *finally* found a fellow sicko and enthusiast. That wasn't entirely true. I was there more for research, to investigate an aspect of my character that confused and baffled me. I am rarely ever titillated by violence or sex. At least repulsion would be a definable emotion.

I first met Leon online, on a forum for people who have depraved inner desires. I don't necessarily fit into this category because I don't have *desires* as such - maybe curiosities. I certainly never enjoyed death and sex, but I am ambivalent to them.

This void in me was the curiosity, not the depravity itself.

Esbjörn wheeled a portable TV on a stand over to his desk and told us to sit down. I saw three CCTV feeds with images of women and men being cut up and abused in torture chambers. I felt absolutely nothing.

Leon reached behind him and pulled out a tape from the rack, forwarded it to Esbjörn. The fat janitor put the video in the player and he leaned on his desk as if observing some great work of art.

The channel buzzed static for a few minutes before it cracked into life – a boy, naked, cuffed to a bed. I heard a chainsaw firing into life off-shot. The only noise more ear-piercing than his screams came from the insane seagulls perched on the railings outside. I watched the entire sordid display.

It's probably the worst thing I've ever seen. I caught my reflection in the convex mirror. I saw the horror of freedom and responsibility. I dream of that mirror every night.

I knew it was wrong, knew I was in the company of the worst people vomited into existence. But watching the horror of mutilation unfold, did I feel sympathy or disgust? No. Just a learned response. I hadn't winced once. Even Leon watched through screwed up eyes towards the end. I felt a tear well in my ducts, scurry down my left cheek. I was not sad for the victim on the screen, I was sad for myself. Nothing.

The victim of numbness.

I move through life like a dismal flame, lath thin.

How did I end up here?

The truth of the matter is that I had always been much too nervous to ever go near Stockholm. It smells of bygone nightmares. There was an old factory. The owner, Mr Hell, was a crapulous old man who shot dogs and stole children. I heard the birds howling under the blisterbright sun, mocking me.

It's such a cliché to say you're a sociopath who wishes

they had a heart. Like the fucking tincan-man begging the wizard behind the curtain to fill a hole in his hollow chest with the absent organ.

People will say things in movies like, *'you want a heart? You don't know how lucky you are not to have one.'* As if all you need are your wits about you to survive. I have a brain. I'm reasonably intelligent, but I know a brain will not bring me happiness. By all accounts happiness is the greatest thing in the world. Even Veronica Jogo in the nursing home tasted happiness at one point. Even Henrik Winslow smiles when someone mentions drums, and he's got conduct disorder.

So I wasn't greatly affected by the snuff movie I watched in the janitor's storeroom with Leon and Esbjörn but there are a few images that're burned onto my mind, a few scenes of such extreme violence that I'm fascinated to an extent by the lack of humanity involved. And to videotape it?

Is that the same as caring - the fact I can't stop thinking about the footage? I don't think I can articulate any definable emotion or opinion one way or the other. I say that 'I know it's wrong' but that's just what society has told me is wrong. What I should say is - ' I know The People think child murder is wrong'. I need to find the man who made that video, assuming he's still alive.

I wonder if he has ever been in love, ever been loved?

Remember, my sentimental friend, a heart is not judged by how much you love but by how much you are loved by others. Sappy bullshit.

The man with the chainsaw in the snuff movie, I remember his eyes so well - my own eyes. Your eyes maybe. Have you ever looked into the eyes of a killer?

Until now of course. I sometimes wonder what people must see when they look into my eyes. Are they oblivious to my callous emptiness, or is the ugliness of my soul apparent to all who squint through their own reflection long enough?

How do people react to you?

Do they see your lack of depth?

I think the truth is that no one cares either way. People who make copious eye contact are doing so in accordance with some human interaction ritual. They aren't looking for anything, not really.

I've never killed a child with a chainsaw but if society caught onto my lack of emotional depth or empathy I'd be punished in the exact same severe fashion. Especially in this fucking city.

But the snuff movie star lives here. I am determined to find him. I'm fortunate that most people don't care enough to penetrate a stare that isn't their own. It's for the minority out there who CAN be bothered scratching the surface that I'm attending these acting classes.

I'm quiet and pale too. I don't have many hobbies or interests. The last thing I remember being passionate about were marbles.

What had once been a living planet was now a long mud hued tube shaped object snaking through the vast cold universes until it swirls and swirls around the void of the black hole like a toilet that will not flush. Excrement that searches for that singularity....

Why does everyone else have memories except me?

I look at Henrik, tall as a set of traffic lights, and try to figure him out. Of course I know that will prove ultimately fruitless; to try and work out someone who has no ulterior motives or need to connect on an emotional level is impossible.

There is simply nothing to understand. The man has no content to speak of. He's a robot - *or an alien, whatever.* As long as Henrik can starve himself of his murderous 'curiosities' he might be of use to us.

I don't think there's any threat he'll decide to switch to Dunwoody's side halfway through our journey. He could kill me in a second and I know I'll have to bargain my way out of his hotel room. Henrik isn't done talking.

'I used to go to drama class every Tuesday night at the old community center. The lecturer there, he was okay, I think he was some ex-soap star whose character got killed off in a house fire. I don't think he ever got over losing that job - his career certainly never recovered. I hoped these classes would teach me how to act like a normal man. Maybe the fucking buzzards will leave me be if they see me pretending to be an upstanding citizen. Maybe not. That's all I want, to be normal, but I know that can't happen, so I'll have to settle for the illusion of normality, a facade that keeps me hidden from the dark watches of a suspicious night.'

'Drama classes really helped?'

'Not really. "Sven" was a leathery tanned guy whose hair had gone this ancient shade of grey. He sat and told us about the Meissner technique, humming and hawing about this and that like some languid philosophical sloth. He did say one thing that stuck - the key to good acting is to 'live truthfully under imaginary circumstances'. If I can just work out how to live 'truthfully' I'm positive I can fit in man. I was always at a disadvantage to the rest of the students in my class because living truthfully was second nature to them.'

I notice the big Swede has no reflection on the cabinet mirror. *A vampire?* Although he wears shabby clothes, Henrik is lean and elegant, like a wealthy impresario or Scandinavian aristocrat.

I look at Anja. Her complexion shines with a blue cosmetic. Her body slotted neatly into the cast iron grooves of the tub.

I can tell Anja had worked at a bargain store or was involved in retail. She was on a zero-hour contract. Her life was a succession of depressing set-pieces, her soundtrack was the groaning sprockets of the boredom and misery factory. I'm sure she preferred death.

'She looks like someone I know.' – I say, observing the bloody mannequin resting beneath the murky depths.

'We all see what we want to see, man.'

I shoot Henrik a scornful glare.

- *What is that supposed to mean?*

'Are you suggesting I want to kill the love of my life?'

'Everyone wants to kill their one true love. If humans have taught me anything it's that. It's the only permissible type of killing.'

What does *he* know, huh? He hasn't even met Kad. I could never hurt her – *never*. Christ, I felt so bad when I thought I'd endangered her back at the Aerial Hotel that I exiled myself to The Schism! Does that sound like someone with a homicidal disposition to you?

Fuck you Henrik.

Fuck your supplies.

'This is silly. You're a murderer. I can't talk to you. I can't bargain with a murderer. And for the record, you know nothing about me or Kad.'

Henrik stands up, towering over Anja and I. I feel like my outburst may have damaged the chances of an alliance. I better calm down.

'I haven't killed for pleasure before Johnny, but I can sure kill for the sake of survival. If you tell anyone I'm here, I will kill you. I'll kill your friend too. So play nice.'

I stand up and meet his chest at eyelevel.

- Sit down 'Kurt'…

'Listen, you don't scare me…'

- Pfft, what a bald-faced lie.

'I *should* scare you. I'm a killer mate, an honest to God killer. It's who I am. I could kill you, easy peasy, and feel *fine* about it afterwards. You couldn't kill someone in self-defence, could you Johnny boy?' – Henrik's voice has lowered to growl.

'But you won't kill me, will you? You won't kill me because all you want is to feel something Henrik. If you kill me you'll have proved nothing.'

'Nice try, but one more body doesn't make a difference, especially if he's an ailing invalid like you. Hell, I killed Anja and I was dating her.'

- Get out of here you fucking idiot!

'Keep your supplies Henrik. I'll take another floor. I'll leave you in peace. Just let me get back to Kad.'

'You don't want any of my supplies?'

'No.'

- You fucking idiot. Kad will kill you if she finds out.

'Henrik, please…'

'Please what? Please don't kill you?' – He horselaughs and shows me a glimpse of the cruelty he masks so well from the rest of society.

'I'm leaving and you're going to let me leave.'

'Is that a fact?'

'Hey, if you really want to feel something Henrik, why not give yourself up to Dunwoody? I see more humanity and hope in the eyes of The People than I do anyone else around here who says otherwise.'

- I can't believe those words just came out of my mouth.

'Because I want to achieve it on my own terms, without accepting a new God into my heart. Anyway, Dunwoody is a false messiah if ever I seen one. I'll chance it on my own.' – Henrik puffs out his chest. I hear the beloved marbles chiming together in the pocket of his tracksuit.

'Maybe. All I know is you know as much as I do and that isn't much.'

I get up and go to leave the bathroom. *As if it'll be that easy to evacuate this situation?* A long arm shoots across the horizon, blocks my exit. In the mirror I see my skin has changed, the pores seem enlarged, my flesh patterned with the deep streaks of accelerated aging. I noticed it earlier. I'm aging. If not aging, then I'm reaching an end-point of some description.

A conclusion.

A climax.

- A surrender?

A younger, pixelated replica observes from behind two-way crystal, waiting for his chance to pounce.

Then a hand clenches a hunk of my hair from behind and yanks it backwards until my neck cracks and my legs buckle. My back smashes into the iron bowl of the tub. The brass glove slips off and lands on the bathroom tiles with a heavy clunk.

Henrik brings out a thumbscrew compass.

- *Fuck...*

He opens the legs of the instrument, setting to a precise radius.

'I need your glove Kurt. I'm building something here, can't you see that? I have an entire floor of supplies that'll last me for months. The People have got nothing on me. I'm sorry, I just can't trust you humans. Fuck your utopia.'

The knot of bone on my wrist has a tender bruise gone the colour of black tupelo. I think it might be fractured too because whenever I go to touch the bone poking out at a wrong-angle, raw nerves flare up and tighten my sphincter. Henrik almost has me.

He throws back his hand with the compass in it, needle-point down-facing, and I prepare for the inevitable sharp pain of being gouged.

Billy Ackerman, Ailsa, the little kid in JAVVA LOTUS, they're all victims of the city's indifference. It denied them the opportunity to ever become anything other than a minor character.

And, of course, the very notion of a Utopia is a selfish one, the people who strive for its existence are ruthless and single-minded. Communism will always lead to totalitarianism, right? Henrik knows this, but I know it too.

My eyes are clenched so tight I can see shapes of light

hurtling towards me. This is it. This is how I go, at the hands of a crazed, marble-obsessed Swedish serial killer. Then I feel a heavy weight tear through the air, smashing against the iron bath before landing in a bundle on the bathroom tiles. I open my eyes. Henrik is lying prostrate on the floor, a puddle of black tar leaching from an entry wound at the back of his skull. I look up. Kad is standing there holding a woodcarving mallet. She looks at Henrik's slumped body and says -

'Found your supplies asshole…'

The woman is a master of the pithy one-liner.

Kad helps me to my feet. I hug her willowy torso, nuzzle her bosom like a child reunited with his Freudian mother until she initiates the separation of our bodies with a subtle cough and a pat on the back.

'Easy there buddy.' She says and squeezes my shoulder to show she's happy I'm alive. I turn to take one last look at the dead girl in the tub but Anja is gone - as if Henrik managed to dump a litre of acid over her, dissolving her to a pool of tooth fillings, before anyone had a chance to double check the detonated corpse.

- That sneaky…

One thing Henrik said to me has fixed itself between the dim bays of my neural galleries.

'To live truthfully under imaginary circumstances'.

I guess he'll never find his snuff movie director.

Some journeys end. Not everything has to be so fucking Kafkaesque!

***

This is a humanistic work. He watches from the pinnacle of the citadel.

Out in the hall Kad and I load up as much as we can of the late Henrik's hidden materials – and it's quite a treasure trove let me tell you.

Henrik had bottles of $10 alcohol and soft drinks stored in the adjacent suites. That's not to mention all the candy, cookies, crackers, and other snacks he'd pugged away for a rainy day. He wasn't kidding either when he said he had saved up enough stuff to last him for months. Kad and I are set. Finally some good luck.

Famous last words, *right?*

We bag all the toiletries and spare clothes, make round trips back to our original floor. Before long room 295 looks like a factory stockroom. Kad pockets a load of condoms too, decides that if we don't both make it out of the city alive then she's going to go out the way she came in – partying and fucking without discrimination. I don't know *what* this means for me or our relationship.

I've been thinking, I possess sensitiveness to beauty and resent anyone who even implies otherwise. I am a good man, yet I walk around this city with a broken heart – how is this possible? I haven't even tested its capacity for love, and it's broken already.

Love is an intruder when it comes to survival.

- Maybe she'll get so caught up in her hedonistic frenzy that she won't notice how pathetic and in love with her I am. Maybe we could share each other's bodies and have done with it? I don't know...

'Hey, look at this...' – Kad hollers from down the corridor. She's looking into Henrik's bathroom. Maybe Anja's corpse has made a miraculous reappearance? When

I get there I see Kad has clearly had the stuffing knocked out of her, she loses her self-possessed edge. There are several bottles of Clorox bleach, household chemicals and concentrated sulphuric acid inside the cupboard beneath the sink.

It's the acid.

'You okay?' – I ask, knowing full well she's *not* okay. Why do I persist on asking dumb questions? Is it a life goal of mine to be considered utterly useless and irritating?

'See that? Acid. I'm going to die here, just like in my dream.'

'Hey, come on!'

'I can't explain it. I feel like that fucker, I feel like he's going to kill me.'

I observe the sprawled Swede.

'Kad, that's impossible. Henrik is dead! You smashed his goddamned brains in back there.'

'I know but…' – Kad looks at Henrik's supine corpse. I can tell she notices the absence of any reflection on the tiles or in the reservoir of black tar merging around either side of his skull.

'We have to dispose of the body.'

'What? Why?'

'Because I can't have him here! We have to get rid of him! We have to get rid of him *right now*!'

I grab Kad and pull her into my chest. I feel her body convulse and her tears moistening my neck but she doesn't make a single whimper.

- Gracious even in hysteria.

Whatever premonitions she's had about her own demise at the hands of Henrik the Terrible, the least I can do is put her mind at ease once and for all.

107

'We're in this together. After all, aren't we both just tiny parts of some greater mechanism, like a chain-spoked carousel of torture and misery?'

'Well that's comforting.'

'I'm not trying to comfort you, just letting you know that you're never alone.'

The stainless walls of PLATOS GATE reflect the number 295. I see the number in the blue lagoons of Kad's teary pupils. Someone is going to die soon. I pray to *something* that it's me.

- I always thought vengeance was unworthy of an enlightened society?

We strip the corpse and go about heaving Henrik's long, skinny body into the empty bath tub. I notice he has no areola and a strange genital atrophy. *Maybe he was an alien?* Kad doesn't waste any time seizing the sulphuric acid and upending its contents over the big Swede's body. She has the corpse fully doused. This maybe isn't the time to tell her that lye and water would've dissolved the body much faster. Why split hairs about something like *this*!

'It's done. Now we wait for him to liquefy.'

'These things usually take a couple of days…' – as the words escape my mouth, I'm astonished to see the acid melt right through the dearly departed alien being before me.

- No way is that human.

I see Henrik's armour burn away little by little. I can't help but notice just how thin his layers are once you penetrate the initial blancmange of skin – that circuitry of tendons and deep tissue beneath look so utterly insubstantial. But that's just one of the myriad flaws in Henrik's creator's rushed, shoddy design.

I hear an audible sigh of relief from Kad's direction.

'You okay?'

'When there's nothing left of him I'll be okay.'

Kad looks as if she's standing face to face with the ghost of herself. We both watch as the flesh around his arms and neck go coal black and flicker to a red sheet of underlying muscle.

A heavy dosage of reality hits me when I least expect it – what are we doing? Is this what life is now? Dissolving bodies to appease our own paranoid delusions?

- It's the way it's always been. One swim in the industrial digester and you're ready for home. Nothing changes, not even the shade of my 5 o'clock shadow.

I wonder if there are any more people on this floor. The city is inducing bad dreams to its citizens. I suppose by giving us paradise this allows those in charge to infringe on our basic democratic rights. I wonder how many people are in this hotel. Is it so much to ask that someone comes along we can actually trust?

Kad and I have no one else but each other. I should be jumping with joy. Fifteen minutes later and Kad deems the puddle of tan liquid that used to be Henrik sufficiently unthreatening. Time to leave…

- We trod forth.

We take the elevator back up to our room. Kad and I do not speak but I fantasise about stimulating the neck of her cervix. I overlay her face onto Ailsa's body and recreate the wild scenes in the bridal suite from before.

Is this love or is this something else?

All I know is that whenever I'm around Kad I

compulsively chew the hangnails from the fingers on my good hand.

When the access parts we both note that the door to room 295 is slightly agape.

- Shit…

There doesn't appear to have been any forced entry. Kad and I can hear the chaos from inside. She stands in the lobby, seemingly frozen in her shoes. I've never seen her like this before.

Is her mind still stuck on Henrik?

Has it thrown her for a loop?

Fuck, maybe she's testing me?

Okay. Time to step up, Kurt. You never thought this day would come but Kad needs you. This is a chance to do something useful for the first time in my sorry existence. I push the door open with the flat of my palm and see the trespasser raiding through our newly acquired supplies.

I grab an umbrella from its cast iron stand. I hold it, ferrule facing forwardly, with tight determination – one hand on the crook-handle, the other just above the ball-spring. I move slowly into the room, my own sharp intake of breath resounding in my ears. I stick two of Henrik's water pills in my mouth and curse my high blood pressure.

I can tell he is built from the stooped posture, those protuberant traps and swollen deltoids that could crush the dimensions of a Volvo truck into a cube of compacted metal. *Christ.* Across the broad canvas of his back I can make out various skin eruptions and cysts. I need to suck it up.

- Come on!

'Hey' – I shout in his direction to get attention, and then I dive at him, drop the umbrella; wrap my arms around his waist. He goes down like a sack of old machine parts and we both crash into the kitchenette area.

He snarls and scratches at me – his face, a bucket of smashed crabs, twists at me, but I look into his eyes and see the dismal flame of hope. Two suns going nova.

I wrestle on top of him, shift his weight.

I take one big swipe at the air beneath me and my brass glove slashes his right cheek to a paper-chain of blood – and in doing so, delivering a much needed blow to the complex literary heritage of his kind.

He yowls and I supply him with the killer blow, stabbing at the throat with two central claws over and over until I feel the warmth of his viscera on my knuckles. I extinguish the dismal flame of hope. My first fatality.

I hear faint sobbing. *Kad…*

'I left the door open. This is my fault…'

'Kad, relax!' – I pull her close and I feel her squirm until I release her again.

'No, I need to be punished!'

'No!'

'Yes, please…'

'Never. Now that's enough. Pull yourself together!'

Kad takes a moment, gathers her emotions and stops sobbing like a child. She looks at me intensely for a minute, a tiny orb of saliva resting on her bottom lip.

'You mean…you *aren't* going to exile me?'

'No.'

'But…I exiled you…'

'Things are different.'

'How are things different?'

'Because I'm in charge now. All your dumb rules are out the window.'

It occurs to me that we will never be free from this place unless one of us faces the creator. While I must admit the thought of being cooped up with Kad in a well-stocked bridal suite does sound appealing, I know she deserves better than that. This is *my* fantasy, not hers.

You see, I know she doesn't love me, could never love me. The truth is that I haven't earned love yet - from *anyone*.

I need to do something meaningful. I need to get Kad out of this hell-hole city and away from Miles Dunwoody. It's time to obtain some meaning, something that transcends mere survival.

What about freedom and happiness?

Meaning requires validation from a locus external to the self.

If I can get Kad to safety maybe that'll unlock the truth – and I really want the truth, no matter how awful it might be.

<u>Seven</u> -

'I dream of a grave, deep and narrow, where we could clasp each other in our arms as with clamps, and I would hide my face in you and you would hide your face in me, and nobody would ever see us anymore.'
— Franz Kafka, The Castle

The burning eye of the sun covers everything in a sort of radioactive yellow. Time to end the recurring dreams of antiseptic metal mirrors and the cityscape that threaten the sensitive souls among us like great silos of acid…

A naked man shambles around the streets, drawing attention to himself with his junked-up jittery, needle-hungry glower. As he searches for the elixir, everyone else just watches. He won't last five minutes on The Schism.

Every organ is visible beneath the diaphanous skin. I turn away.

Wind howls in from the northeast. Distant screams sore heavenward. While hunting the shadows, I see a body spotlighted, sagging limply from a lamppost. A woman gone flaccid - *Ailsa.*

There is no time to stare, no time to mourn. I mean, she and I shared nothing beyond physical gratification, I need to keep that in mind. It's amazing how quickly the onset of love can snuff all those Darwinian urges to fuck and repopulate. It's liberating to silence the inner demon of lust, even if it is just temporary.

- Christ, you sound like Miles fuckin' Dunwoody himself!

Squash all impure thoughts, chase things that are innocent and pure!

I'm no fundamentalist but there's something to be said for finding meaning in interpersonal relations with other human beings. This whole nightmare has been one long journey to connect with someone. I'm wearing Kad down. I think, I hope, she has a new respect for me. I think Kad finds me magnanimous, fair-minded, loving even. These are traits I aspire to hold and project. In this sense I have had a successful life, albeit short and full of violence.

I move through the shadows, away from Ailsa's dangling corpse.

If Kad knew what I was doing, that I'd left her to go track down Dunwoody, she would fucking kill me – and leaving her wasn't easy. For the duration of my descent through the intestines of the PLATO'S GATE hotel I was in constant conflict, between my craving to get answers for Kad and the desire to stay and protect her to the best of my ability.

Now I'm on the streets, I'm not entirely positive what my next step will be. Wait for Dunwoody and The People to come get me? *Then what?* What if they convert me? I just know that there's no use in just waiting around.

No, I don't exactly have a full proof plan to work with, just a burning incentive to do something right for someone I love. It's not my wish that you think me noble, but I do want to be remembered, even just in the mind of an onlooker like yourself, as a well-intentioned and halfway proactive protagonist.

Not quite a hero, but, at least, a man.

For the first time, a notch of stars. It's like daylight outside. Lanterns hang from the cedars. This city doesn't need darkness, it is a self-contained evil.

An old woman stands hunch-necked on the street corner holding a popcorn crate with vials of sparkling plum-coloured solution. From her coin headscarf and her various accoutrements I can tell she possesses a supernatural conception of good and evil. She has one eye but spots me lurking and tells me to approach.

'I'm not one of The People, but I, um, feel I should warn you they are on their way.'

'How can you tell?'

'I have a sense for these things. I'm an artery of the city, we're *all* connected. That's why, um, that's why they will inevitably find you Kurt. In this place, we're all the same. Whoever you used to be, it doesn't matter.'

'I have no memories of who I used to be, but I'm full of guilt. How do you explain that?'

'No idea, I'm not a mystic – well, no more of a mystic than you. That is to say, your guilt must be inherited from the communal conscience, though negative feeling usually is. There are a lot of bad people in this city who want redemption. A lot of guilt has been alleviated by Dunwoody but it stays hovering in the air like a layer smog. The guilt is infectious if you breathe it in. Don't, um, never breathe it in, no, no…' – she says this like someone struggling to organize their caffeinated thoughts. She conforms to the chaotic rhythm of details within the city.

'I hate The People. They're always telling me I'm an animal.' – I say this staring off into the pseudo-blue sky.

'Oh, now, we can't judge The People. I mean, I'm a Jew. I am. A Jew. Of course it is not MY belief that Jews are all money scrounging victims, but I, um, I must respect that it might well be someone else's opinion, you know?

As an educated woman it's my duty to, um, at least to respect it. You see, I don't AGREE with it, but I RESPECT someone else's right to express it.'

'But they don't just express it, they enforce it with bloody vigor! I don't have to respect someone who tells me I'm a goddamned animal. If we go by your method then I have just as much right to express distaste towards the People as they do to dark dwellers.'

'I'm sorry but you're wrong. You don't have the right, not yet.'

'Excuse me?'

'I can see you, the real you. The real. You. You're like a big ball of pink goo filled-out with guilt and fear instead of the normal stuffing humans have inside them.'

'There's more to me than guilt and fear lady. There's love too.'

'Yes. But that alone doesn't entitle you to the right to call yourself human. Let me tell you something about guilt, it is all consuming. You have to, you *have* to, shed it if you want to be a person. I remember, a long time ago, um, I, uh, had become embroiled in a defamation case. My editorial about students being cry-babies was retracted from the university newspaper. They felt it violated basic routine journalistic practices. A deposition was sought by, um, by attorneys, it was all very embarrassing. I consider myself a rebel in my own way. How I ended up here? Well, I guess it's a funny story. It had such an innocuous beginning, as these things usually do.

'I walked into the kitchen one morning and saw my husband was already up, his legs sticking out from the cupboard under the sink. There were a bunch of hand tools strewn across the lino. I went about preparing things for breakfast, as I'd grown accustomed; figured he was tightening one of the loose pipe fittings – he *hated* to be harassed when he was trying to be handy. He saw every innocent inquiry I made as an expression of doubt regarding his ability to achieve masculine tasks.

'I got out the eggs, cracked them into a bowl of milk and butter. Stuck two, um, two slices of brown bread into the toaster slots and started whisking. It was then I realised my husband wasn't tightening anything. I realised this wasn't necessarily even my husband. I saw an unfamiliar hand bringing out elbow joints of pipe. Upon closer inspection, it became apparent that the two log-like legs didn't belong to Brian either. *Someone* was dismantling the plumbing system.

'Next thing I know, I'm stuck in this place. *But*, I've reformed my thinking *without* the help of Mr. Dunwoody. I'm much more, uh, open-minded and I came to that destination on my own terms. They leave me alone. I never get any hassle. The key is acceptance of who you are.'

'But I don't fucking know who I am!'

'Course you do. You're you!' – She looks at me monocularly.

I hear a rope snap and the sound of a deadweight thumping the tarmac. I can't bring myself to look. I *know* we didn't love each other, but I couldn't stand to see Ailsa in that state, like a casualty of war left by the roadside to rot in a heap. The old woman looks over though and barely reacts. She looks at me and smiles a vacant grandmotherly smile.

'I remember Ailsa's husband, um…what was his name? Um, oh, Joe. That's it. He was a Construction

117

Management undergrad when I knew him. A guy who drops the 'R' at the end of every syllable. Joe was an easy guy to like. He was also head of the, uh, the, uh…the Afro-American Cultural Centre. Some people thought he was a hyperactive dilettante, oh yes. Meeting that new wife of his didn't help. That's how Ailsa wound up here. But she couldn't change. She was too damn stubborn.'

She shuffles on the spot, her sturdy legs and overripe figure undulate as she attempts to stifle an itch. It's so hot that the blood tickles the raised veins beneath the skin of my forearms.

A klaxon sounds and Dunwoody's robotic voice emerges from the rooftops of every building in a refrain of condemnation -

… *And the sun died again in a sky like black smoke. Year 295, the year of the Consulship of Tuscus and Anullinus.*

'Be thankful for the clouds, Kurt, for they are a veil that hides the truth.'

'You thought yourself safe, untouchable, but the beast is merciless. Nothing you do will stir sympathy in its heart… vast beyond measure, it has no more regard for your suffering than the human species has for an insect's. You are less than an ant … a source of humour for the beast. And when it sees your eyes projecting that tiny cult image of god onto the infinite cosmic canvas…

'As the feeble light of your dead world burns its final ember, the agony will have only just begun…'

The old woman and I communicate with our eyes - I go for trepidation but it's impossible to tell exactly what's going on in her head.

'That doesn't sound very promising. Tell me, before I go, what is the significance of the number 295?'

She takes a moment, gapes at me like a lobotomized idiot, like one of The People.

'Well, the angel number 295 is a sign that you should trust and love yourself much more than you're doing right now…'

- Fucking hell.

'Never mind.'

'You remind me of a Bermudan writer called Trout. He wrote 'Barring-gaffner of Bagnialto', 'Maniacs in the Fourth Dimension' and a bestselling memoir, 'My Ten Years on Automatic Pilot'. He turned science fiction plots into jokey little parables, was quite obscure and died poor.'

'I think he sounds familiar.' – I reach into the cloud of names and characters hovering above the city and find Trout's name and his creator.

'I hope you won't take offence to this but you seem kind of half-rendered. I can't quite put my finger on it.'

'Not at all.'

'Hey, you know what? Where I'm from originally, well, we lived in a wonderful age of technology. People who didn't have the nerve to kill themselves had this new outlet, a form of therapy called The Simulacra.

'There's a company called - well I can't actually remember their name, but it's a conglomerate acronym of some description – they created these droids that look exactly like you, act like you too. Then, uh, they put you in a room with the replica and let you do or say whatever the hell you want.

'So, um, you can kill the droid. You can just yell at it. It'll take any amount of abuse you throw at it. All it costs is one simple piece of information. It has to be delicate. It has to be important information. Something you were trusted to keep, something only the alien government could benefit from. I remember, I think, I remember I told the company about my father's little side business dispensing controlled substances to bipolar patients, a crime worthy of 60 years' incarceration in the cities of Wire and Shell County. I knew exactly what the consequences would be and, sure enough, on February, The State Drug Task Force served a search warrant at the offices my father worked and the results of the investigation were presented to an SS Federal Grand Jury.'

'So you sold your own father up the river?'

'Do I feel bad about what I've done to my father? Yes, a little. Remorseful. That's too extreme a word. There was no room for proselytism in my father's world. Anyway, that was a long time ago and he's dead now. He's somewhere else entirely.'

'I think we're from different places originally.'

'Immitants use liquid-cooled electronic motors to power themselves, it also gives them the capacity to learn introspection and rational thinking. A Simulacra robot is less complex, less able to learn. It lacks the recursive self-improvement of ultra-intelligent machines. It is born as an adult but has the understanding of a small child. She is a child lost in a chaotic supermarket. Worse than that, she is like a heroin baby - a child of inherited affliction. This city would gobble up that version of me in a heartbeat.'

I turn to leave, convinced this geriatric fool can't help me, when she grabs me by the inner arm.

'I can sell you a memory.' – She says. This time I can tell she's trying to communicate a seriousness with her eyes.

'How?'

'Easy. You just take this potion before you go to sleep every night. It'll manipulate your dreams and completely re-build your sense of self. The black fluid is added to animal blood which acts as a potent hallucinogen and hypnotic.'

'Huh. Can I choose the memory?'

'That's the snag. Because it's such an unstable formula, synthesized from the most random and volatile properties, you kind of just have to accept the luck of the draw.'

'I'll take it.'

'Here you go.' – she passes me a vial.

'What do you want in exchange?'

'Nothing. What use is money here? Currency doesn't exist! These vials are as close to legal tender, they're the only thing that can be exchanged for happiness and escapism. If you tell me one thing that's been on your mind for the longest time. Relieve some of your burdensome load. Tell me something you haven't previously had the courage to say…show me some courage.'

'I thought you knew everything anyway. I thought we were all connected, no secrets and all that?'

'Just indulge me, please, indulge, indulge…'

'Okay…I wish I could tell Kad I love her.'

'Good. That's perfect. Enjoy your dream.'

She passes me a copy of the poetry journal New Coin.

'Some reading material. I'm in that you know.' – She says a little smugly.

'Really.'

I hand it back to her. I won't rise to the old woman's

efforts at making me jealous.

'You're in it too.'

There is a spasm of, what must be, pride that transcends all my previous acts of heroism. I take back the magazine and observe the dog-eared page. Sure enough, there's the name 'Kurt' above a poem about an antique city.

- I'm published?

'I don't even remember writing this.'

'That's because, um, you *didn't* write it. I did. I guess that means you get some of the credit too, even though you appear to be subliterate. When I look at that page I see a poem about Harvard students picketing outside a university building. The name says Octavia, not Kurt. We see through our own eyes.'

'Can I keep this?'

'Yes, I suppose so, if you really like the feeling of being published, sure. You like this feeling eh? There's an Evergreen Review, issue 295 I think, I have it somewhere in my backpack. It says I wrote an essay about the South African poet Sinclair Beiles, but it'll probably change title and author to suit you. Your eyes will rearrange the information. That's what happens here. This city is one big collective nightmare.'

'Goodbye Octavia.'

***

I find a blind alleyway running between two of the stately conglomerate buildings. I take my crewneck off and place it on the level patch of dirt and grime. The alleyway is a runnelled cave, this is the perfect spot.

Overhead powerlines crackle with life. They're close. I don't have much time.

I feel the encumbrance of fatigue on my mind and body, making my limbs all dense and my muscles achy.

I'm ready to melt into a silver puddle.

A bracket of bollards keep me hidden behind a long cast shadow. The People can't take this last dream away from me. I rest my back on the labyrinth of utility ducts running up the side of the metallic structure, tilt my head and wait to be enveloped in warm sleep.

The filth covered semi-permeable concrete is cold beneath my buttocks, even through the fabric of my crewneck…

It's okay though. It's almost…

Almost time…

For a real rest…

To dream and…

To learn who I once was.

Embrace the artificial reverie.

All I can do is pray it's a damn good one. Pray there are no mirrors in sight.

I remove the cork and flex my nostrils over the lip of the vial. Smells like bologna. I swig back the purple potion. It tastes kind of like fizzy soda, it bubbles in the throat, goes down scratchy. All I have to do now is find a quiet place to go to sleep and dream.

Maybe my attitude should be '*I'll dream when I'm dead. Once I find Dunwoody and try to set Kad free*', but I'm tired. And, hey, perhaps I've even earned it. There shouldn't be a big price on earning a decent sleep free of psychological anxiety.

I can't shake the premonition. My god is a merciless god who hates all his creations equally. The dark throne above all those mountains of bone. The bones of women. I open the issue of New Coin and glare proudly into my name until the letters become blurry.

This will be like my last meal before execution.

I'd risk dying just to dream a happy song.

A group of men in lab coats are talking like grand ayatollahs behind a glass screen. They see me looking in and someone draws a pair of venetian blinds to shut out our view.

A dustcart drones across the decaying tenements lined up along the opposite side of government headquarters. The glass and metal has given way to crumbling stone.

Our orange moon simmers in the reeking haze.

The dream…I have a memory embedded in the back of my skull. A memory of a human life half-lived. I am practically a boy in this memory, in this dream - A guy, a glamorous crook - like a young John Dillinger or Baby-Faced Nelson.

I was walking up to the cash desk. I put down a can of Coke and some bubble gum on the counter. I don't think I had any intention of paying for the items.

The clerk was an old Asian man who looked at me suspiciously over his spectacles while he scanned through each item. We were the only two people in the store.

'2.95' – he said.

I started rooting around my pockets, pretending to search for change. I still had no intention of paying.

Then, my hand met the cool, metal haft of the cooking knife buried deep in the thick goosedown dimensions of my puffer jacket. The clerk was leaning on the desk, still looking at me over both hemispheres of his spectacles.

'2.95!' – he said, aggressively this time.

I took a deep breath and went to jerk out my weapon. What the fuck was I thinking? Suddenly the sensory door chime went off and someone entered the shop. I panicked and fled towards the door. The clerk called after me a few times – '*Hey! 2.95! 2.95!*' – but I got away safely into the street and round the corner into the alleyway without being pursued. I think I was a shitty person, a sad and lonely person.

At least I was a person. I get outside and meet a girl with dark hair. The majority of the dream is taken up by our sexual exploits. We seek union in beds and on floors, against walls, in the cramped spaces of Cinquecento's and beach coves—we'll fuck anywhere on offer, this dream girl and I.

I'm certain I'm lousy at it even in the dream. But she keeps coming back for more. Like she loves me anyway.

My mother continues to smear her reflection with Windolene.

My father continues to eat with his mouth open.

I have an old brown car, a Cinquecento. I've had it for years and it remains unblemished. I think that it was never a great car but it got me from A to B and served me well during my time among the dream-living—nothing too ostentatious.

Then I'm in a basement. It smells dry, as if all the wood rot and moisture accumulated throughout winter has been absorbed into something else. Sparks fly out from the breaker panel, partially illuminating the dim basement. Then I see it. The beast of the final act.

I'm standing with a phone to my ear…

I pick up the telecom receiver and dial in the code. My hands are sweaty, I hear my own hyperventilating in the echoey mouthpiece. Straight away I get a muzak version of

126

Harry Nilsson's 'Without You'. The elevator music cuts suddenly and a nasal voice emerges.

Chris Kelso

Eight -

Nothing is true, everything is permitted.
- William S. Burroughs

Heat from the filtered sun beats down. Smells of metal and alloy. The whispers from the light create a cool breeze on the back of my neck. I wake up, shoot a ceilingward gaze. The familiar sense of dread returns.

It's impossible to wake up in a city like this without a true, overshadowing sense of your own mortality. I can't help but feel we missed the initial stages, we weren't organised enough. We should've banded together sooner, while the uprising was insipient.

Instead we waited. That's why we lost. That's why we'll never win. Never.

- How long was I out?

I don't feel any different. I achieved a memory, a sense of self and yet I feel utterly empty. Perhaps emptier than before.

'You…'

I look upwards and see Dunwoody is standing atop the open-air roof deck of the 72-storey bank tower. He flickers like a hologram, wearing a cableknit pullover and filling the bowl of a corncob pipe with synthetic opioid.

'Are you ready to listen now my little firecracker?' – He takes a puff.

I am worn-out by his whitewash, each loss chips away a new part of my soul leaving an irreplaceable gap. I've been set up by Octavia. My copy of New Coin is nowhere to be seen.

'You resisted long enough. You proved your point.'

'Have I?'

'Yes. You should know that the black fluid that bleeds from everyone is from a blown capacitor on the power supply or motherboard. This place is coming down, we're going with it unless you join me. The insects are on their way. If you think this place is bad…just wait.' - All that's left inside is raven blackness, my insides have been scraped clean. I can't handle another defeat.

'I know you think my attitude displays an un-comradely cynicism, but please tell me what I am.'

'You are not a man, but you're not an animal either. Hackers know you as Bandookay Ray, a backdoor virus created on the 2nd of September 2005 who attacks the Windows family. You took out four of the company's main computers and they hold this against you to this day. That's why they're sending the beast. You now exist within the mainframe of the RAD750 Processor units. You were created by BrianII, RyanII, ZionII and LionII. They are my friends. We're the same, you and me. We're both viruses. You just happen to be a virus who writes poetry.'

'I'm published.'

'If you are published then you should believe in miracles. I am your designer, or the cities designer. Decoding signals from the retina, that's all the scientists are doing. They played every B-movie you can think of and recorded their neuron firings. The city is a projection of an old science fiction movie. You and I, we have enzymes but not hormones. Hormones require target cells, which viruses lack. You could inhibit my body and together we could bring down the scientists from the inside, then all the people of the city would be finally free.' – He exhales a spiral of blue vapor.

'You don't want freedom Dunwoody. Freedom is the end of your existence. Without the humanized suffering of slaves, you serve no purpose. You're like Al Green or Hitler, the progression of human society does not interest you. You need the conflict, otherwise you'll die.' – Dunwoody reaches out and touches me with his hand, bumpy as a cat's tongue. I withdraw my claw but feel the phantom sensation of a fully-digited limb. My hand. Five fingers.

An arbitrary gesture from the Lord?

- 1, 2, 3, 4, 5 fingers… but wait…

Dunwoody's face is impassive, like he never even heard me.

'No. No, I don't need you. I could easily let you all kill each other, stay here to suffer, but I am the mother. You will do as you're told. I have written on holy …'

'Mandatory speeches will kill us all. All I have to do is walk away.' - Rage continues building up inside my body like air being furiously pumped into a deflated football. My mouth is full of the hot dust of eternal noon.

'And go where? I exist simultaneously in many worlds.'

I take a deep breath.

'You know, I never just sat down and thought about it. About why you care so goddamn much about what I think and do. And, well, I'll be honest with you, Miles, I don't buy for a second that you're some hyper intelligent computer virus who *thought* us all into fucking existence. I'm sorry, my brain just can't untangle that into something that's plausible – but I do believe you're some kind of gnostic demon, maybe a demiurge, who has fallen in love with humanity, or the idea of humanity at least. The problem with that is, that in the moment you grant a vessel sentience, when you offer it humanity even as an illusion, you can't then hope to control it.

'You see it's as good as human, there's no half measure. There is no half past fucking human. You try your best to control us in different ways, callous and cruel ways that aren't on a level playing field. I mean, you try to control those of us who were animals by making us fear your power as the dominant species. You do that well – the occasional exhibition of wrath here, the odd possession of an innocent there…

'You seek to terrify those of us who were once human by putting the fear of god into their hearts. By trapping us in a nightmare and forcing us to look at ourselves until we hate the sight of our own reflections. But Miles, did you know that love is really the key to power, control and happiness? I mean, like, really. It sounds so fucking trite, but it's true. Equipped with love, real love that can go unrequited because its content just existing on its own, I can see through all your deception. All of it.

'If you *are* my mother and we are all lying in your giant womb, then I must say, I *reject* you mother. I do not love you. How could I love such a monster? Its love you seek, I know it is. That's what every living thing with sentience wants. I bet you didn't expect one of your little science experiments to achieve it before you, eh? I have the power now Dunwoody so you'd do well to back the fuck away. I don't need you to protect me from the darkness anymore or from the beasts that lurk within it. That's not what being alive is all about. You have to show a little bravery. Arm yourself with love. Let someone inside. Fear is the mind killer, and the highway to fear is the shortest route to defeat.' – A tear the colour of cucumber juice, translucent in diluted green, runs down the course of his chiselled cheek.

'I'm very disappointed in you Johnny. If you refuse to co-operate I have no other option than to let the beast get you. He's on his way. If you cannot achieve light then there is simply no hope for you. You persist on dwelling in the darkness. The beast feeds on darkness. Why?'

'Because Kad dwells here.' - While I feel like I have indeed mastered my fear, I can still taste the molecules of my own sweat.

Kad and I share the same locus of consciousness, separated only by body, time and place. She is my ghost sister. I feel inextricably connected to her, she's the only person who intimately knows how I feel, knows the real me.

'You know we made this world, not you? This is *our* world, the one we wanted, where meaningful things happen all the time and it's more like a work of fiction than any kind of reality that's gone before. If we made this world, and *I* made the beast, then surely we're just as capable of destroying this world and pulling apart the sinews of the fucking bogyman prowling in the shapes of our dark home? You want me to believe I'm trapped in some taxonomical system, stuffed and docile but once dangerous and mobile. So I'll take the memory of a streetpunk who tried to rob a convenience store. It is what it is. You have to accept your lot in life, what gives us the God-given right to anything better? Happiness has to be

133

earned, I know that now. You appeal to the entitled. I don't want to look into the past, I don't really have a past to look back into. I do have a future though. It can be whatever I choose it to be.'

'You think you know it all.' – He mocks.

'I know you're not human.'

'That's not true. As viruses we are half supra molecular complexes and half biological entities. We behave like bacteria, more complex even than biochemical mechanisms.'

'…and have you forgotten about the other monsters, like the parasitic life-form that assimilated organisms into its giant, gelatinous bulk; then there was the extra-terrestrial with convex eyes and tentacles that tore gateways to awful universal extra-dimensions; or what about that phantom with the mechanical arm, slotted eyes and metallic teeth that tormented each member of your family with complex philosophical questions? The beast that's coming is ten times worse – skin desiccated, pulled thick-tight over poles and splinters of bone, an array of eyes bleeding down itself.'

'Really?'

'The beast has serrated teeth across the entire surface of its hide that chomps repeatedly, *instinctively*. Six-foot-long tentacles poke out from its layered abrasive and flaps wildly. It could skin you. Now as the blubber envelopes the whale precisely as the rind does an orange, so is it stripped off from the body precisely as an orange is sometimes stripped by spiralizing it. Page 295.'

'This beast wants revenge?'

'The beast hates all of you. It will swim through the vellum-thin walls of this city and devour you all, starting with you. The funny thing is that you created it, you and the rest of your dark dwellers. You-ou-ou-ou-ou…' – his electrolarynx appears to catch on the word 'you' and trail off in a hideous siren of vowels. The tears have interfered with his circuitry. I knew the illusion would be ruined if he continued to malfunction like this in my presence. Love is evanescent.

Part of Dunwoody's ugliness, what makes him so detestable, stems from the preservation of the uncanny.

'This will be a pyrrhic victory Kurt.' – he says finally.

Dunwoody starts to clog on his grief and sounds like a cat hawking up a hairball or a dog about to vomit. The thought of killing him in my heart and mind has wrung out my adrenal glands.

- I'm not Ahab at all. I'm the fucking whale. But, please, call me Ishmael…

In my mind I looked up to bear witness to the fragile creatures flight. Only in my mind.

<u>Nine</u> -

'...to the last I grapple with thee; from hell's heart I stab at thee; for hate's sake I spit my last breath at thee.'
— Herman Melville, **Moby-Dick**

What is the conclusion? Miles Dunwoody has been and gone from my life. Now I have a life left to leave with, what do I do with it? I sense the struggle isn't over just yet.

I have these faint criss-crossing scars on my wrists. I wasn't trying to kill myself, just trying to feel something other than complete sadness. It didn't work. No one found me and I never cut deep enough to sever any arteries. Didn't stop me making a habit of it.

I use a shard of glass to cut the alphanumeric symbol tattooed on the witches into my arm. I finally proved myself. I'm finally worthy. Or I'm about to be at least.

In the mirror of my mind my flesh is the off-pink pallor of liverwurst; my doughy features are as inhuman and unsympathetic as the cosmic entity which awaits me.

Kad puts a tab of rat poison on her tongue, rivulets of mascara streaming down her cheeks. I do the same. Her confidence has returned, tough as shrapnel. Her anaemic complexion holds all the light I'll ever need.

We walk out into the railed parapet and gaze into an ingot ocean of oil. At our inverted reflection.
- I'll never get out of this fucking place any other way…
I prepare to swallow. I hear Kad gulp. Ripples break

the symmetry of my reflection. I see in the distance, a traveller huddled at the prow of a...

- Is that a ship?

I look beside me and Kad is gone, but when I contemplate at the unsettled water I see her sanding right next to me. Is this a dream? If it is, then the water holds my dream's structure.

I refuse to ever look up from the reflective mirror into the polished monitor. Whoever or whatever I was, it doesn't matter anymore. I will keep dreaming, even if in doing so, my ship evaporates into the dust of imagination.

We're getting *exactly* what Dunwoody thinks we deserve. Sick and forgotten in the south of nowhere...

To my left there's a busted up old warehouse with kids inside playing around with chemical drums and shards of broken glass—seem happy enough. The rippling surface of the sea looks serene. It's too distant to be real. Nothing pleases me anyway.

I'm stuck in this crumbling city. Rather in here than out there among the street-smart living dead. I rest my stomach on the glass balustrades, lean over to inhale the grease-sea. The surface of water undulates. Maybe there's something beyond.

A typhoon is headed southwards. I can hear the great whale who bit off my fingers thunder just beneath the surface of the oil. The beast writhes under the surface and emits a shriek of such celestial suffering that Kad and I both experience the true isolation of the universe in the quarries of our soul, if only for a brief moment. I'm stumbling towards a dénouement here.

I gaze into the offing. What do I expect to see?

My greatest foe.

My son.

I'm ready for him. I'm ready to belong.

'Spending practically every minute of your day on pure survival is an absolutely boring life.'

- Samuel R. Delany, *Neverÿon*

ABOUT THE AUTHOR

Chris Kelso is an award-winning genre writer, editor, and illustrator from Scotland. His work has been translated into French and he is the two-time winner of the Ginger Nuts of Horror Novel of the Year (in 2016 for 'Unger House Radicals' and in 2017 for its sequel 'Shrapnel Apartments'). 'The Black Dog Eats the City' made Weird Fiction Reviews Best of 2014 list.

THE BLACK ROOM
MANUSCRIPTS VOLUME
THREE

Chris Kelso features in *The Black Room Manuscripts Volume Three* with his short story **The Cloud Sculptors Of Hachimantai**, co-written with Preston Grassmann.

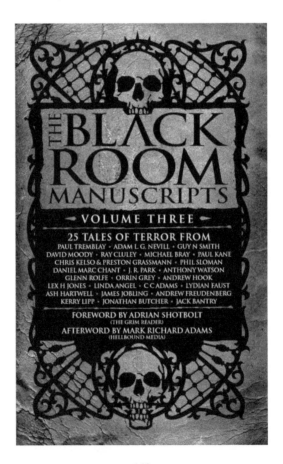

THE BLACK ROOM MANUSCRIPTS VOLUME THREE

Some words are born in shadows.

Some tales told only in whispers.

Under the paper thin veneer of our sanity is a world that exists. Hidden just beyond, in plain sight, waiting to consume you should you dare stray from the street-lit paths that sedate our fears.

For centuries the Black Room has stored stories of these encounters, suppressing the knowledge of the rarely seen. Protecting the civilised world from its own dark realities.

The door to the Black Room has once again swung open to unleash twenty five masterful tales of the macabre from the twisted minds of a new breed of horror author.

The Black Room holds many secrets.

Dare you enter…for a third time?

.

The Sinister Horror Company is an independent UK publisher of genre fiction founded by Daniel Marc Chant and J R Park. Their mission a simple one – to write, publish and launch innovative and exciting genre fiction by themselves and others.

For further information on the Sinister Horror Company visit:

SinisterHorrorCompany.com
Facebook.com/sinisterhorrorcompany
Twitter @SinisterHC

SINISTERHORRORCOMPANY.COM